"Why didn't y

"He teleported straight to Dzur Mountain."

"Dzur Mountain," I repeated a long moment later. "Well, I'll be dragon fodder. How could he have known the teleport coordinates? How could he have known he'd be safe from what's-her-name? How—?"

"Her name is Sethra Lavode, and I don't know."

"We'll have to send someone after him."

"No chance, Vlad."

"Why not? We've got money."

"Vlad, it's *Dzur Mountain*. Forget it."

"What's so special about Dzur Mountain?"

"Sethra Lavode," said Kragar. "She's a vampire, a shape-shifter, holds a Great Weapon, is probably the most dangerous wizard living, and has the habit of killing people who get near her, unless she decides to turn them into norska or jhereg instead."

"There are worse fates than being a jhereg, boss."

"Shut up, Loiosh."

I said, "How much of this is fact and how much is just rumor?"

"What's the difference if everyone believes the rumors? I know I won't go near the place."

I shrugged. "Then I'll have to go myself."

STEVEN BRUST, PJF

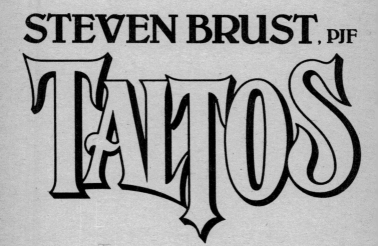

TALTOS

ACE BOOKS, NEW YORK

This book is an Ace original edition,
and has never been previously published.

TALTOS

An Ace Book / published by arrangement with
the author and the author's agent, Valerie Smith

PRINTING HISTORY
Ace edition / March 1988

ISBN: 0-441-18200-3

Ace Books are published by The Berkley Publishing Group,
200 Madison Avenue, New York, New York 10016.
The name ''ACE'' and the ''A'' logo
are trademarks belonging to Charter Communications, Inc.
PRINTED IN THE UNITED STATES OF AMERICA

10 9 8 7 6 5 4 3 2 1

Acknowledgments

My thanks to Nate, Emma, Kara, Pam, and Will.

Special thanks are due Gail Bucich for help in keeping my history straight, and thanks, as always, to Adrian Morgan.

To Fluffy

1 □

The Cycle: Dragon, dzur, and chreotha; athyra, hawk, and phoenix; teckla and jhereg.

They danced before my eyes. The Dragaeran Empire, its population divided into seventeen Great Houses, each with its animal representation, seemed to unfold in my hands. Here was the Empire of Dragaerans, and here was I, the Easterner, the outsider.

It wouldn't get any easier.

The eyes of no gods upon me, I began.

Some two hundred miles to the north and east of Adrilankha there lies a mountain, shaped as if by the hand of a megalomaniacal sculptor into the form of a crouching grey dzur.

You've seen it, I'm sure, in thousands of paintings and psiprints from hundreds of angles, so you know as well as I that the illusion of the great cat is as perfect as artifice or nature could make it. What is most interesting is the left ear. It is fully as feline as the other, but is known to have been fabricated. We have our suspicions about the whole place, but never mind that; we're *sure* about the left ear.

1

It is here, say the legends, that Sethra Lavode, the Enchantress, the Dark Lady of Dzur Mountain, sits like a great spider in the center of an evil web, hoping to snare the true-hearted hero. Exactly why she would wish to do this the legends don't make clear; as is their right, of course.

I sat in the center of my own evil web, jiggled a strand, and caused it to bring forth more particulars about mountain, tower, and lady. It seemed likely that I was going to have to visit the place, webs being the fragile things that they are.

Of such things are legends made.

I was going over a couple of letters I'd received. One was from a human girl named Szandi, thanking me for a wonderul evening. On reflection, I decided it had been pretty nice at that. I made a mental note to write back and ask if she'd be free sometime next week. The other was from one of my employees, asking if a certain customer could have an extension on a loan he'd taken out to cover gambling losses to another of my employees. I was thinking about this and drumming my fingertips when I heard Kragar clear his throat. Loiosh, my familiar, flew off his coat rack and landed on my shoulder, hissing at Kragar.

"I wish he'd stop doing that, boss," said Loiosh psionically.

"Me, too, Loiosh."

I said to Kragar, "How long have you been sitting there?"

"Not long."

His lean, seven-foot-tall Dragaeran frame was slouched in the chair opposite me. For once, he was not looking smug. I wondered what was bothering him, but didn't ask. If it was any of my business, he'd tell me. I said, "Do you remember a Chreotha named Fyhnov? He wants to extend his loan from Machan, and I don't know—"

"There's a problem, Vlad."

I blinked. "Tell me about it."

"You sent Quion to collect the receipts from Nielar, Machan, Tor—"

"Right. What happened?"

"He scooped them up and ran."

I didn't say anything for a while, I just sat and thought about what this implied. I'd only been running this area for a few months, since the unfortunate death of my previous boss, and this was the first time I'd had this sort of problem.

Quion was what I call a button-man; an ambiguous term which in this case meant he was responsible for whatever I wanted him responsible for from one day to the next. He was old, even for a Dragaeran—I guess close to three thousand years—and had promised when I hired him that he'd stopped gambling. He was quiet, as polite as Dragaerans ever are to humans, and very experienced at the sorts of operations I was running—untaxed gambling, unlicensed brothels, making loans at illegal rates, dealing in stolen goods . . . that sort of thing. And he'd seemed really earnest when I'd hired him, too.

Shit. You'd think, after all these years, I'd know better than to trust Dragaerans, but I keep doing it anyway.

I said, "What happened?"

"Temek and I were protecting him. We were walking by a shop and he told us to wait a minute, went over to the window like he wanted to look at something, and teleported out."

"He couldn't have been snatched, could he?"

"I don't know of any way to teleport someone who doesn't want to be teleported. Do you?"

"No, I guess not. Wait a minute. Temek's a sorcerer. Didn't he trace the teleport?"

"Yeah," said Kragar.

"Well? Why didn't you follow him?"

"Ummm, Vlad, neither of us has any interest in following him where he went."

"Yeah? Well?"

"He teleported straight to Dzur Mountain."

"Dzur Mountain," I repeated a long moment later. "Well, I'll be dragon fodder. How could he have known the teleport coordinates? How could he have known he'd be safe from what's-her-name? How—?"

"Her name is Sethra Lavode, and I don't know."

"We'll have to send someone after him."

"No chance, Vlad. You won't convince anyone to go there."

"Why not? We've got money."

"Vlad, it's *Dzur Mountain*. Forget it."

"What's so special about Dzur Mountain?"

"Sethra Lavode," said Kragar.

"All right, what's so special about—"

"She's a vampire, a shape-shifter, holds a Great Weapon, is probably the most dangerous wizard living, and has the habit of killing people who get near her, unless she decides to turn them into norska or jhereg instead."

"There are worse fates than being a jhereg, boss."

"Shut up, Loiosh."

I said, "How much of this is fact and how much is just rumor?"

"What's the difference if everyone believes the rumors? I know I won't go near the place."

I shrugged. Maybe if I were Dragaeran I'd have understood. I said, "Then I'll have to go myself."

"You want to die?"

"I don't want to let him get away with—how much did he take?"

"More than two thousand imperials."

"Shit. I want him. See what you can learn about Dzur Mountain that we can count on, all right?"

"Huh? Oh, sure. How many years do you want me to put in on this?"

"Three days. And see what you can find out about Quion, while you're at it."

"Vlad—"

"Go."

He went.

I settled back to contemplate legends, decided it was pointless, and began composing a letter to Szandi. Loiosh returned to his perch on the coat rack and made helpful suggestions for the letter. If I thought Szandi liked dead teckla, I might have even used some of them.

Sometimes I almost think I can remember my mother.

My father kept changing his story, so I don't know if she died or if she left him, and I don't know if I was two, four, or five at the time. But every once in a while I get these images of her, or of someone I think is her. The images aren't clear enough to describe, but I'm sort of happy I have them.

They aren't necessarily my earliest memories. No, if I push my mind back, I can recall endless piles of dirty dishes, and dreams of being made to wash them forever, which I suppose comes from living above a restaurant. Don't get me wrong; I wasn't really worked all that hard, it's just that the dishes made an impression that has stayed with me. I sometimes wonder if my entire adult life has been spent in an effort to avoid dirty dishes.

One could, I suppose, have worse goals.

My office is located in back of a psychedelic herb shop. There's a room between the shop and the office that houses an almost continuous shereba game, which would be legal if we paid taxes, and would be shut down if we didn't bribe the Phoenix Guards. The bribes are less than the taxes would be, and our customers don't have to pay taxes on their winnings. The office portion consists of a set of several small rooms, one of which is mine, another of which is Kragar's. I have a window that will give me a wonderful view of an alley if I ever decide to unboard it.

It was about an hour after noon three days later when Kragar came in, and a few minutes after that, I suppose, when I noticed him sitting there.

I said, "What did you find out about Dzur Mountain?"

He said, "It's big."

I said, "Thank you. Now, what did you find out?"

He pulled out a notebook, flipped through it, and said, "What do you want to know?"

"Many things. To start with, what made Quion think he'd be safe going to Dzur Mountain? Was he just getting old and desperate and figured what the hell?"

Kragar said, "I've reconstructed his movements for the past year or so, and—"

"In three days?"

"Yeah."

"That's fast work for a Dragaeran."

"Thanks too much, boss."

Loiosh, perching on his coat rack, sniggered into my mind.

"So, what were you saying about his movements?"

"The only really interesting thing I found was that about a month before he started working for you he was sent on an errand to a certain Morrolan."

I chewed this over, then said, "I've heard of Morrolan, but I can't remember how."

"Big-shot wizard of the House of the Dragon and a friend of the Empress. Lives about a hundred and fifty miles inland, in a floating castle."

"Floating castle," I repeated. "That's it. The only one since the Interregnum. Bit of a show-off, then."

Kragar snorted. "To say the least. He calls the place 'Castle Black.'"

I shook my head. Black is, to a Dragaeran, the color of sorcery. "Okay. What does Morrolan have to do with—"

"Technically, Dzur Mountain is part of his fief. It's about fifty miles from where his castle usually is."

"Interesting," I said.

"I wonder how he collects taxes," said Loiosh.

"It's the only thing that stands out," said Kragar.

I nodded. "Mountains have a way of doing that. But all right, Kragar. It's a connection, anyway. What else do you know about Morrolan?"

"Not much. He spent a good portion of the Interregnum out East, so he's supposed to be tolerant of Easterners." Easterner means human, like me. But Dragaerans call themselves human, which is plainly ridiculous, so it can get confusing.

I said, "Well, I could start with visiting Morrolan, if he'll consent to see me. What did you find out about Dzur Mountain?"

"Bits and pieces. What do you want to know?"

"Mostly, does Sethra Lavode really exist?"

"She certainly did before the Interregnum. There are still accounts of when she was a regular at court. Deathgate, boss, she was Warlord more than once."

"When?"

"About fifteen thousand years ago."

"Fifteen thousand years. I see. And you think she might still be alive? That's, what, five or six times a normal life span?"

"Well, if you believe the rumors, fledgling heroes from the House of the Dzur like to chase up the mountain every so often to fight the evil enchantress, and they're never heard from again."

"Yeah," I said. "But the question is, do we believe the rumors?"

He blinked. "I don't know about you, Vlad, but I do."

I ruminated on moldy legends, enchantresses, dishonest button-men, and mountains.

"You just can't trust anyone anymore," said Loiosh who flew down onto my right shoulder.

"I know. It's a sad state of affairs." Loiosh snorted psionically. *"No, I mean it,"* I said. *"I trusted the son of a bitch."*

I took out a dagger and started flipping it. After a while I put it away and said, "All right, Kragar. Send a message to the Lord Morrolan, asking him if he'd deign to receive me. Whenever he wishes, of course; I'm not—say! How do you get there, anyway? I mean, if it's a floating castle—"

"You teleport," said Kragar.

I groaned. "Okay. Try to set it up, all right? And get the coordinates to Narvane. I don't feel like spending the money on the Bitch Patrol, so I'll just live with a rough ride."

"Why don't you do it yourself, then?"

"Not *that* rough."

"You getting cheap, boss?"

"What do you mean, getting?"

"Will do, Vlad."

Kragar left the room.

Now that I have a few years' perspective, I have to say that I don't think my father was cruel to me. The two of us were alone, which made everything difficult, but he did as well as he could for who he was. And I do mean we were alone. We lived among Dragaerans, rather than in the Eastern ghetto, so our neighbors didn't associate with us, and our only other family was my father's father, who didn't come to our side of town, and my father didn't like bringing me to Noish-pa's when I was an infant.

You'd think I'd have gotten used to being alone, but it hasn't worked that way. I've always hated it. I still do. Maybe it's an instinctive thing among Easterners. The best times were what I now think must have been slow days at the restaurant, when the waiters had time to play with me. There was one I remember: a big fat guy with a mustache and almost no teeth. I'd pull his mustache and he'd threaten to cook me up for a meal and serve me with an orange in my mouth. I can't think why I thought that was funny. I wish I could remember his name.

On reflection, my father probably found me more a burden than a pleasure. If he ever had any female companionship, he did a good job of keeping it hidden, and I can't imagine why he would. It wasn't my fault, but I guess it wasn't his, either.

I never really liked him, though.

I suppose I was four years old before my father began taking me regularly to visit my grandfather. That was the first big change in my life that I remember, and I was pleased about it.

My grandfather did his job, which was to spoil me, and it is only now that I'm beginning to realize how much more he did. I must have been five or six when I began to realize that my father didn't approve of all the things Noish-pa was showing me—like how to make a leaf blow slightly askew of the wind just by willing it to. And, even more, the little slap-games we'd play that I now know to be the first introduction to Eastern-style fencing.

I was puzzled by my father's displeasure but, being a contrary little cuss, this made me pay all the more attention to Noish-pa. This may be the root of the problems between my father and me, although I doubt it. Maybe I look like my mother, I don't know. I've asked Noish-pa who I resemble, and all he ever says is, "You look like yourself, Vladimir."

I do know of one thing that must have hurt my father. One day when I was about five I received my first real beating, which was delivered by, I think, four or five punks from the House of the Orca. I remember that I was at the market running an errand of some sort, and they surrounded me, called me names I can't remember, and made fun of my boots, which were of an Eastern style. They slapped me a few times and one of them hit me in the stomach hard enough to knock the wind out of me; then they kicked me once or twice and took the money I had been given to make the purchases. They were about my own size, which I guess means they were in their late teens, but there were several of them, and I was pretty banged up, as well as terrified of telling my father.

When they were finished with me, I got up, crying, and ran all the way to South Adrilankha, to my grandfather's house. He put things on the cuts that made me feel better, fed me tea (which I suspect he spiked with brandy), brought me home, and spoke to my father so I didn't have to explain where the money had gone.

It was only years later that I actually got around to wondering why I'd gone all the way to Noish-pa's, instead of going home, which was closer. And it was years after that when I got to wondering if that had hurt my father's feelings.

About twenty-two hours after Kragar left to set things up, I was leaning back in my chair, which has a strange mechanism that allows it to tilt, swivel, and do other things. My feet were up on the desk, crossed at the ankles. The toes of my boots pointed to opposite corners of the room, and in the gap between them Kragar's thin face was framed. His chin is one that a human would call weak, but Kragar isn't—that's just another one of his innate illusions. He is built of illusions. Some natural, others, I think, cultivated. For example, when anyone else would be angry, he never seems to be; he usually just appears disgusted.

The face that was framed in the V of my boots looked disgusted. He said, "You're right. You don't have to take anyone with you. What interest could a Dragonlord possibly have in hurting a poor, innocent Jhereg, just because he's an Easterner? Or should I say, a poor, innocent Easterner, just because he's a Jhereg? Come on, Vlad, wake up. You have to have protection. And I'm your best bet for avoiding trouble."

Loiosh, who had been swooping down on stray lint, landed on my right shoulder and said, *"Just point out that I'll be there, boss. That should keep him from worrying."*

"You think so? What if it doesn't?"

"I'll bite his nose off."

I said aloud, "Kragar, I could bring every enforcer who works for me, and it wouldn't make any difference at all if Morrolan decides to shine me. And this is a social call. If I show up with protection—"

"That's why I think I should come. He'll never notice I'm there."

"No," I said. "He's permitted me to visit. He said nothing about bringing a shadow. If he did notice you—"

"He'd understand that it's policy in the Jhereg. He must know something about how we operate."

"I repeat: no."

"But—"

"Subject closed, Kragar."

He closed his eyes and emitted a sigh that hung in the air like an athyra's mating call. He opened his eyes again. "Okay. You want Narvane to do the teleport, right?"

"Yeah. Can he handle the coordinates?"

"Morrolan said one of his people would put them straight into the mind of whoever we want to do the spell."

I blinked. "How can he do that? How can one of his people achieve that close a psionic link with someone he doesn't know?"

Kragar yawned. "Magic," he said.

"What *kind* of magic, Kragar?"

He shrugged. "How should I know?"

"Sounds like witchcraft, boss."

"That's exactly what I was thinking, Loiosh."

"You think he might be employing a witch?"

"Remember, he spent a lot of time out East, during the Interregnum?"

"Yeah. That's right."

I flexed my fingers. "In any case," I said, "I do want Narvane to do the teleport. I'll want him here tomorrow an hour ahead of time."

Kragar nodded and looked bored, which meant he was unhappy. Loiosh was going to be unhappy, too, pretty soon.

Them's the breaks.

2 -

I began laying out what I would need for the spell. I concentrated only on my goal and tried not to think about how silly it was to arrange tools, objects, and artifacts before I had any idea how I intended to use any of them. I let my hands pull from the pack various and sundry items and arrange them as they would.

I couldn't know what I'd need, because the spell I was about to attempt had never been performed before; didn't even exist—except that I had to do it now.

I arrived at the office too early the next day. I'm good at waiting patiently when I have to, but I don't like it. It would be hours before I was due at Castle Black, and there was nothing at the office that required my attention. I puttered around for a while, pretending to be busy, then said, "Screw it," and walked out.

The orange-red sky was low today, mixed with grey, threatening rain, and the wind was in from the sea. I walked, or actually strolled, through my area. These few blocks of Adrilankha were mine, and a certain satisfaction came with that knowledge. I stopped in to see a guy named Nielar, my first boss and then one of my first employees.

I said, "What's new?"

He gave me kind of a warm smile and said, "Business as usual, Vlad."

I never know how to take Nielar. I mean, he could have had the position I hold if he'd been willing to fight a bit, but he decided he'd rather stay small and healthy. I can respect that, I guess, but, well, I'd respect him more if he'd decided to take the chance. What the hell. Who can figure out Dragaerans, anyway?

I said, "What have you heard?"

"About what?"

"Don't give me that."

If he'd played dumb a little longer I'd have bought it, but he said, "Just that you got burned by one of your button-men. Who was it?"

"It doesn't matter, Nielar. And it'll matter even less in a little while."

"Right."

"See you."

I walked out of Nielar's shop and headed toward South Adrilankha, the Easterner's ghetto.

Loiosh, sitting on my left shoulder, said, *Word is getting around, boss.*

"I know. I'm going to have to do something about it. If everyone thinks I can be taken, I will be."

I kept walking, thinking things over. With any luck at all, Morrolan would be able to steer me toward Quion. Would he be willing to? I didn't know.

"Going to visit your grandfather, boss?"

"No, I don't think so. Not today."

"Then where? No, don't tell me. A brothel or an inn."

"Good guess. An inn."

"Who's going to carry you home?"

"I'm only going to have one or two."

"I'll bet."

"Shut up, Loiosh."

"Boss, you are going to Castle Black, aren't you?"

"If I can work up the nerve. Now let me think."

It started drizzling about then. I drew on my link to the

Imperial Orb and created an invisible shield, setting it up over my head. It was an easy spell. Most passersby I saw had done the same. The few exceptions, mostly of the House of the Teckla, headed for doorways to wait it out or else got wet. The streets became very muddy, and I made a mental note to allow time to clean my boots. There must be sorcery that can do that. I'll have to learn it one of these days.

By the time I had crossed Twovine and entered South Adrilankha the rain had stopped, which was just as well. Very few Easterners are sorcerers, and I didn't want to call that kind of attention to myself. Of course, I was wearing the grey and black of House Jhereg, and Loiosh riding on my shoulder was enough to proclaim, "Here is a witch!" but there was no need to make matters worse.

About then, Loiosh caught something of my thoughts and said, *"Wait a minute, boss. Just who do you think you're leaving behind?"*

"You, chum. Sorry."

"Crap. You can't—"

"Yes I can. One does not bring a jhereg to visit a Dragonlord. At least not on a first visit."

"But—"

"You're not expendable, you're not stupid, and you're not going."

This gave us something to argue about until I reached the place I was looking for, which helped distract me. The thing is, I was really terrified. I very badly wanted not to go, but I couldn't think of any way out of it. I tried to picture myself showing up there and I couldn't. Yet, if I didn't follow up on Quion, my reputation would suffer, and, in the Jhereg, reputation means money and safety.

I found Ferenk's, which was right where I'd been told it would be, and I stepped inside, pausing to let my eyes adjust to the relative darkness. I'd never been there before, but my grandfather had recommended it as *the* place to find good Fenarian brandy.

One thing that shed a great deal of light on how Dragaerans think was when I realized that they had no term for brandy, even though they had the drink. They called it wine, and, I guess, just had to know the bottler to decide how strong it was and what it tasted like. To me, brandy and wine aren't even close in taste, and maybe they aren't to Dragaerans, either. The thing is, Dragaerans don't care if they taste different, or that the process of making one has almost nothing to do with the process of making the other; the point is, they are alcoholic drinks made from fruit, so they must be the same thing. Interesting, no?

Easterners don't have that problem. Ferenk's especially didn't have that problem. One entire wall behind the long, dark, hardwood bar was filled with different Fenarian brandies, about half of them peach. I was very impressed. I hadn't known there were that many in existence. I was very glad that the Empire wasn't currently at war with Fenario.

The place was pretty much empty. I licked my lips and sat down at a tall, high-backed chair right at the bar. The host glanced at Loiosh, then wiped the counter in front of me and looked an inquiry.

I glanced at the peach brandies and said, "A glass of Oregigeret."

He nodded. "Dead bodies and seaweed, eh?"

I said, "Is that what you call it?"

He shrugged. "Well, it isn't what I'd call gentle."

I said, "What do you recommend?"

He glanced at the wall and picked out a short, round bottle and showed it to me. The label was faded, but I could see the lettering, which read "Barackaranybol."

I said, "Okay. I'll try a glass of that."

He pulled out a glass, reached under his counter, and put some ice into it. My first reaction was to be impressed that he could afford to buy the ice, not to mention the spells to keep it cold. Such things aren't cheap around here. But then I realized what he was doing and I said, "No, no. I don't want ice in it."

He looked disgusted. He pulled out a pitcher, filled the glass with water, and pushed it in front of me. Then he poured some brandy into another glass and set that next to the water. He said, "I'm just giving you some water to clear your mouth out before you drink the brandy. You know how to drink 'em; I know how to pour 'em, okay?"

I said, "Right," to the host, and started to sip the brandy.

I heard Loiosh giggling. *"Shut up,"* I told him. I put the brandy down, took a sip of water, then drank some of the brandy. The brandy was very good.

"I'll have the same," came from right behind me. The voice was low in pitch, velvety, and very familiar. I turned and felt a smile growing on my face.

"Kiera!"

"Hello, Vlad."

Kiera the Thief sat down next to me.

I said, "What are you doing around here?"

"Tasting Fenarian brandies."

The host was staring at her, half hostile and half fearful. I was a Jhereg but at least I was human. Kiera was a Dragaeran. I took a look around and saw that the three other customers in the place were staring at Kiera with expressions that held different mixtures of fear and hatred. I turned back to the host and said, "The lady asked for a drink."

He glanced at the table where the other three humans sat, at Kiera, then back at me. I held his gaze, waiting. He licked his lips, hesitated, then said, "Right," and poured her the same thing he'd given me. Then he wandered over to the other end of the bar. I shrugged, and Kiera and I moved to a table.

"So," I said. "Come here often?"

She smiled. "I've heard that you're having some troubles."

I shook my head. "Someday I'll find out how you learn these things."

"Maybe you will. Do you need help, Vlad?"

"Just courage, I think."

"Oh?"

"You probably know one of my button-men has been stealing the eggs."

"Yeah. And mama hen isn't happy."

"Papa rooster if you don't mind."

"Right. What are you doing about it?"

"Going somewhere I don't want to go, for starters."

"Where?"

"Have you ever heard of Castle Black?"

Her eyes widened appreciatively. "A Dragonlord named

Morrolan, I believe," she said.

"Right."

She cocked her head to the side. "I'll tell you what, Vlad. You go ahead and follow him there. If Morrolan kills you, he won't live out the month."

I felt a lump rise in my throat. After a moment I said, "Going into another line of work, Kiera?"

She smiled. "We all have friends."

"Well, thanks," I said. "That's yet another one I owe you."

She nodded, still smiling. Then she got up, said, "Good wine," and walked out of the place.

And it's funny. Revenge is rather silly. I mean, I'd be dead, why should I care? Yet, somehow, her saying that was just what I needed to reassure me. I still can't figure out why.

I had another drink after she left and, just to prove Loiosh wrong, stopped at two. I called on my link to the Orb once more, and found I still had a couple of hours before I had to be back at the office. I paid the host, told him I'd be back sometime, and headed for home.

My grandfather has a white cat named Ambrus, who is the most intelligent cat I've ever met, as well as the oldest. I never actually played with him, the way people usually play with cats, but sometimes, when a child, I would sit and talk to him while my father and grandfather were in the other room, talking. I used to pretend that he could understand me, and either he really could, or my memory is playing tricks on me, because a normal cat couldn't have responded the way Ambrus did: meowing *exactly* in answer to questions, purring when I told him I liked him, and extending his claws and swiping at the air behind him when I'd point that way and say, "Look out, a dragon."

Knowing what I know now, I don't think my memory is playing tricks on me.

In any case, one day when I was, I don't know, maybe seven, my father saw me talking to him and scowled.

I said, "You don't like cats, papa?"

He said, "It isn't that. Never mind."

I think I remember seeing Noish-pa standing behind him,

watching the scene, and maybe smiling just a little.

Humans do witchcraft, Dragaerans do sorcery. I do both, which is unusual, so I'm in a good position to compare them. The one difference that keeps hitting me is that witchcraft is more *fun*. If a witch could teleport (a thing that seems impossible, but I could be wrong), it would involve hours of preparation, rituals, chanting, and filling all the senses with the desired result until the spell would work in a blinding explosion of emotional fulfillment.

Narvane, one of my enforcers and an excellent sorcerer, just said, "Ready?"

I said, "Yeah."

He casually raised his hand, the office vanished around me, and I felt a lurch in my gut.

There was a day when I did something, I don't remember what, and my father slapped me for it. I probably deserved it. It wasn't the first time he'd slapped me, but this occasion I recall specifically. I think I must have been about seven or eight.

What I remember is that I looked up at him curiously and shook my head. His eyes grew wide, and maybe a little fearful, and he stood there staring at me for a moment before turning and walking into the other room. I guess he wanted to ask about the look on my face, but he didn't, and I didn't say anything. You must understand, I was very young, so I'm reconstructing a lot of this from memory, but I retain the impression that my reaction frightened or puzzled him a little. But what was going through my mind was something like, "You call that hitting someone? That hardly hurt. I get beat worse than that every time you send me to the market for bay leaves."

I didn't notice where I was at first, because I was too busy feeling sick to my stomach. Dragaerans don't have this reaction to teleports but I do, and every other human I know does, too.

I kept my eyes closed and resolved not to throw up. Maybe the brandy had been a mistake. I risked a quick look and saw that I was in an open courtyard; then I realized that I was standing on air and closed my eyes again. Whatever was holding me up felt solid. I took a deep breath and opened my eyes again.

The great double doors of the castle were about fifty yards in front of me. High, high walls were all around. Why did Morrolan have walls around a castle that floated? I risked a look down and saw orange-red clouds. Above me was more of the same. There was a cool breeze on my face bringing a faint smoky smell. I saw no one else in the courtyard.

I glanced around the walls and saw towers placed at the corners. Towers, walls, and the castle itself were of the same black stone—obsidian, I think—much of it carved into figures battling or hunting or just lounging on the walls.

Pretentious bastard.

I saw a pair of guards in one tower. They both wore the black and silver of the House of the Dragon. One carried a spear, the other a staff.

Wizards, employed as guards.

Well, he'd certainly convinced me that he was rich, if nothing else. The guard with the spear saw me looking at him and saluted. I nodded back, wishing Loiosh were with me, and started walking toward the great double doors of Castle Black.

If I look back on my life as if it were that of a stranger, I'd have to say that I grew up around violence. That sounds peculiar to me, because I've never really thought of it that way, but as far back as I can remember I had a fear of Dragaerans. Home was above father's restaurant, which was in an area where Easterners—humans—didn't live. I spent most of my time in the restaurant even before I started helping around the place. And I can still remember the thrill of fear every time I left it, and long chases through alleys, and beatings at the hands of Dragaerans who didn't like humans, or other humans who thought we were getting above ourselves. This latter—being beaten up by other Easterners—didn't happen often. The first time I think I was about eight. My father presented me with an outfit in the colors of House Jhereg. I remember that day because it was one of the few times I can recall seeing my father happy. I picked up his mood and went strutting around in my new clothes and was found by a few human kids about my own age who, well, you can guess. I'll spare you the details.

The funny thing is that I remember feeling sorry for them, because I'd been beaten by Dragaerans, and was thinking that these poor, puny Easterners couldn't even beat me up as well as Dragaerans could.

My boots went *clack clack* against thin air, which was a bit unnerving. Things became even more unnerving as I got closer to the doors and recognized marks around them as witchcraft symbols. I licked my lips.

I was about ten feet away when both doors swung open with great, silent majesty. They didn't even squeak. This was *very* unnerving. I immediately ran one hand through my hair and adjusted the clasp of my cloak with the other. This allowed my arms to brush over various goodies that I conceal about my person because it's better to give than to receive surprises.

But I didn't spend much time thinking about the doors, as there was someone standing in the doorway, framed like a picture by the tall arch. She had the fine, fair skin of the House of the Issola, and wore the white and green of that House in the form of a half gown, half sari. Her eyes were clear blue, her hair a light brown, and she was beautiful even by human standards.

Her voice was low and sweet. "Greetings, noble Jhereg," she said (apparently deciding the term was less insulting than "Easterner"), "to Castle Black. I am Teldra. We have been awaiting you, and it is our hope that you will allow us to make your stay pleasant. I hope the teleport was not too discomforting?"

As she finished this amazing speech, she bowed in the manner of the Issola. I said, "Ummm, no, it was fine."

She smiled as if that actually mattered to her. In fact, I really think it did. She said, "Please, come in at once, and I'll send for the Lord Morrolan." She extended her hand

for my cloak, and I'll be damned if I didn't almost give it
to her, just out of reflex.

My reflexes don't generally work that way.

"Ummm, that's all right," I said. "I'll keep it."

"Of course," she said, smiling. "Please follow me."

It crossed my mind then that she hadn't called me by
name, which probably meant she didn't know how to pro-
nounce my patronymic, which meant that Morrolan probably
didn't know a lot about me. That was most likely good.

I crossed the threshold of Castle Black. I was in a vast
hall, with white marble stairways curling up to my right
and left, a large arched exit before me, smaller ones to the
sides, balconies above me, and a few landscape paintings—
no psiprints— on the walls. At least everything wasn't done
in black.

Then one of the landscapes caught my attention. It had
a huge yellow sun at the upper right and the wisp of white
clouds in the sky. I'd seen such sights before, through my
grandfather's eyes. It was a scene done in the East.

Teldra escorted me through the tall arched doorway in
the center, down about twenty paces of wide, unadorned
but well-lit hallway into what was clearly a sitting room.
The predominant color here was pale yellow, and the room
was filled with overstuffed chairs, buffets, liquor cabinets,
and tables. I gave up looking for potential traps in the first
ten seconds. I wished Loiosh were with me.

Teldra indicated a chair that looked comfortable and af-
forded a view of the door. I sat down. She said, "The Lord
Morrolan is expected in a moment. Would you allow me
to serve you wine?"

"Um, yeah," I said. "Thanks."

She brought a bucket of ice with a bottle in it, which told
me something else; it is the Easterners who serve wine
chilled. She removed the bottle, took the wine tongs from
the coals, expertly circumscribed the neck, dipped the
feather in the ice, and lifted off the top of the neck. All of
her movements were fluid and graceful, as if she were dancing with her hands. She poured and I drank. It was really
very good, which was another surprise. I studied the bottle,

but didn't recognize the label.

"Is there anything else I can get for you, my lord?"

"No, no," I said. "I'm fine. Thank you."

"Until later, then, my lord."

I rose as she left, although I wasn't sure if it was proper. Teldra nodded as if it was, but I suspect that if I'd remained seated, that would have been proper, too.

Dragonlords don't use poison; I drank some more wine. Presently, unannounced save by the rap-rap sound of his footfalls, the Lord Morrolan entered the room.

He was tall and dressed in black, with bits of silver lace on his blouse and on the epaulettes that peeked out under the full cloak he wore thrown back. His hand rested on the hilt of a longsword. His face had the angularity of the House of the Dragon. His forehead was high, and his hair was very dark, straight, and long enough to cover his ears. I gave the sword a second look and realized, even though it was sheathed, that it was a Morganti blade, and powerful. I repressed a shudder as I felt it ringing in my mind.

It was only as an afterthought that it hit me: Why was he wearing a blade—and a Morganti blade at that—to greet a guest inside his home? Could he be afraid of me? Could it be the custom of Dragonlords to go wandering around armed in their own homes, or when greeting guests?

Or was he planning to just haul off and kill me?

You can believe what you like about the existence of the soul, or the Dragaerans' faith in reincarnation. But even if you don't believe any of that, there is no question that if I were killed by a Morganti weapon, that was it for me. I froze for a moment, then realized that I ought to acknowledge his presence, since he, at least, hadn't attacked me yet.

I rose and gave him a half bow. "Lord Morrolan, I am Vladimir Taltos. I am honored that you should consent to see me." I'm a good liar.

He nodded coolly and indicated with his head that I should sit. Teldra returned and poured him a glass of wine as he sat opposite me. As she left, he said, "Thank you, Lady Teldra." Lady? I wondered at their relationship. Meanwhile, Morrolan was appraising me as I'd appraise a jewel. His eyes never left me as he drank. I returned the favor. His complexion was fairly dark, though lighter than a Hawk's or a Vallista's. His hair was black and shoulder-length and curly and just a bit neglected. He sat rather stiffly, as if he were wound too tight. The movements of his head were quick, feral.

Eventually he set his glass down and said, "Well, Jhereg" (apparently deciding the term was more insulting than "Easterner"), "do you know why you are here?"

I licked my lips. "I thought I did. I may have been deceived, of course."

"It is likely," said Morrolan.

"That being the case," I said, falling into his speech patterns, "perhaps you would be so kind as to enlighten me."

"I intend to," he said. He studied me some more, and I began to get the impression that he was doing that just to irritate me, or perhaps to test me—which works out to the same thing.

If you're a Jhereg and an Easterner, you have to expect to be insulted from time to time. If you want to live, you have to learn not to take offense at every slur and sneer. But this was beginning to get annoying. I said, "It seems to me, most noble Dragon, that you were about to tell me something."

A corner of his mouth twitched. "Yes." Then, "A certain employee of yours was traced to Dzur Mountain. You have learned that, some time ago, he paid me a visit as part of negotiating a small land transaction. You are anxious as to his whereabouts. It seems he has run off with the family silver, as the saying goes."

"It turns out," I said, "that I knew that much already."

"Quite. Now, however, you wish to find him to kill him. You can find no one willing to travel to Dzur Mountain, so you thought to visit me, perhaps to learn what I know of the truth behind the legends of Sethra Lavode."

I was beginning to get downright irritated, as well as frightened, by how close his guesses were. I mean, what a pompous, supercilious jongleur. But the thought came to me that he was a pompous, supercilious jongleur with a very powerful Morganti blade, and he was a sorcerer, and I was in his keep. I resolved to stay polite. I said, "It is certainly the case that I am curious about Dzur Mountain, and I would appreciate any information you can give me on it, and its inhabitants."

Morrolan, by this time, was giving me a look that couldn't decide if it was a mild sneer or an attempted scowl. He said, "Very well, Jhereg, a question: Would you like to find this straying employee of yours?"

I spent a moment trying to find verbal traps in the question, then gave up and said, "Yes."

He said, "Very well. Let us go to him."

He stood up. I did the same. He took a step closer to me and seemed to concentrate for just a moment. I realized what he was doing almost at once. I thought about resisting, but made a split-second decision; I might never have another chance. You have to take some risks in any business. I allowed the teleport to take effect. My stomach lurched and the walls vanished around me.

3

The knife went near my right hand, various herbs and things went near my left hand. I didn't yet know precisely which of my supplies I'd pulled out, nor did I want to, but I noted the string with nine knots, the ash twig shaped like a bull's head, the miniature copper kettle, the toe bone of an elk, the piece of braided leather, and a few other things.

I wondered what I'd do with them.

Morrolan said, ''Welcome to Dzur Mountain.''

My stomach said, *Why do you keep doing this to me?*

My knees felt weak and I braced myself against a damp stone wall. We were on a small landing, surrounded by stone, with a single, narrow stairway leading up. High above me, diffuse light trickled in through a tiny window. There was a torch burning on the wall along the stairway, and the soot on the wall above it was old. This place, then, was not used often, but had been prepared.

I hid my discomfort as best I could and said, "Charmed." I did not want to throw up. I repeated this to myself a few times.

Morrolan set his foot on the lowest stair. "This way," he

said. To gain time, I said, "Sethra Lavode?"

"She awaits us."

"Oh," I said. I took a couple of deep breaths and began following Morrolan up the stairs, which were deep as well as narrow, designed for Dragaerans rather than humans. There were many steps. The stairway curved gently to our left. At one point we passed a window and I took the opportunity to look out. We were, indeed, high up in the mountains. If I'd had more time, I think I could have enjoyed just looking, as I caught a glimpse of pine trees and a green valley. There was also snow, however, as well as a cold, sharp breeze that struck me through the window. The chill from it continued up the stairs with us. But my stomach was settling down, so I couldn't complain.

Morrolan continued two steps ahead of me. I decided he must be pretty trusting to walk with his back to me. On the other hand, my eyes were on a level with the hilt of his longsword. This kept my tongue in check for some time. Eventually, however, I risked saying, "With all respect, my Lord Morrolan."

He stopped and turned. "Yes, my good Jhereg?"

"Would you mind giving me some idea as to what, by all the Demons of Terlocha, is going on?"

He smiled an enigmatic smile and resumed his climb. I followed. Over his shoulder, he said, "What do you wish to know, my lord?" There was, I think, a bit of ironic emphasis on the last two words.

I said, "For instance, why did you agree to see me?"

I saw rather than heard a chuckle at that. "It would have been foolish not to, after going to all that trouble."

I'd be lying if I said this didn't send shivers down my back. A few steps more and I was able to say, "So you planned to bring me to you."

"Of course, if we couldn't convince you to come directly to Dzur Mountain."

"Oh. Of course. Foolish of me."

"Yes."

I clenched my teeth and said nothing. The hilt of his blade was still before my eyes, and I could feel its hunger. I shivered.

Then, "All right, Lord Morrolan, you have me here. Why?"

Over his shoulder he said, "Be patient, my lord. You will know soon."

"All right."

I said nothing for another turn of the stairs, thinking about Sethra Lavode. In all probability, I would soon be meeting her. Why? These people had no cause to kill me, and they could have done so already if they'd wanted. What were they after?

I said, "What about Quion, then?"

"Who?"

"The button-man—the employee of mine who vanished in Dzur Mountain."

"Ah. Yes. He was set up, of course. He came across certain information implying that he could expect sanctuary here. The information was incorrect."

"I see."

Another turn of the stairs. "How much farther up are we going, Lord Morrolan?"

"Not far, I think. Are you getting tired?"

"A bit. But never mind." He'd said "I think." I pondered that and said, "So, are you a regular visitor to this place?"

"Oh, yes," he said. "Sethra and I see each other often."

That set me a pretty mystery, with which I was able to occupy myself for another turn or two of that endless stairway. Why was he unsure of the length of the stair if he was often at Dzur Mountain? Obviously because he didn't usually come this way. We passed a heavy wooden door on the left side but didn't stop. Why was he coming this way now? In order to tire me out, or else to size me up, or both.

This realization, which ought to have put me more on guard, actually did nothing except make me more angry. But, with some difficulty, I kept my voice even as I went back to an earlier subject of conversation.

"Lord Morrolan, I think I can understand how it was that you knew Quion would come to Dzur Mountain with the gold."

"I am pleased for you."

"But what I don't understand is how you knew he was

going to grab the money in the first place."

"Oh, that part was easy. You see, I am something of a witch. As are you, I believe."

"Yes," I said.

"Well, then, as you know, with witchcraft it is possible to plant an idea in someone's head. We let it occur to him that it would be a good and safe thing to do, and he did it."

"You bastard!" This burst out of me before I could stop it. I regretted it at once, but it was too late.

Morrolan stopped and turned toward me. His hand rested easily on the hilt of that sword. He looked down at me, and the expression on his face was not pleasant. He said, "I beg your pardon?"

I watched his eyes and didn't answer. I allowed my shoulders to relax and mentally fingered my nearest weapon, a stiletto with a four-and-one-eighth-inch blade, located in my left sleeve and set to draw with my right hand. My best chance was to lunge for his throat. I estimated my chance of killing him to be fairly good if I drew first.

On the other hand, looking at the way he stood—the lack of tension in his neck, shoulders, and arms, and the balanced power of his stance—I guessed that he had very good odds of giving me a cut as I nailed him. And, with a Morganti blade, one cut would do the job.

"Let me put it this way," I said. "If you mess with one of my people again, I'm going to cut your heart out." I let my breathing relax and watched him.

"Are you really," he said, making it more a statement than a question. His face took on a sardonic expression, and with no warning he took a step backward, up another step. Damn, he was fast! His blade wasn't yet drawn, but now I'd have to either try to draw my rapier or throw the knife. Killing someone with a thrown knife, even if you're as good as I am, is more a matter of chance than skill.

I said nothing, waiting for him to draw. He also waited. His knees were slightly bent and his balance was perfect, left foot on the higher stair, right hand on the hilt of that weapon. I felt the coolness of the dagger's hilt press against my left wrist and decided it was my only chance. My rapier may as well have been back home; he was faster than me. I continued to wait.

Finally, he smirked and bowed slightly. "All right, my lord Jhereg, we'll settle this later." He presented his back to me and continued up the stairs. The idea of nailing him came and went. Even if I got away with it, that would leave me in Dzur Mountain, alone except for a very irate Sethra Lavode, who could probably prevent me from teleporting out.

Besides, there was still the matter of Quion and two thousand gold imperials.

I took a helping of nonchalant and followed him. My knees were steady, which took all of my concentration for the next few moments. We passed a couple more doors on the left, then emerged into a narrow hallway. We followed the hallway through an arch, after which it widened. The walls were black and unadorned save by torches. I didn't recognize the stone here, but it wasn't obsidian, in any case. It was rough and seemed to absorb light. Where the black at Morrolan's keep seemed to work hard to be ominous, the black at Dzur Mountain was naturally gloomy and hinted, almost as an aside, at insidious power and dark strength.

Yes, I know that to a Dragaeran black means sorcery. But to me black is gloomy. Dragaerans are warped; I've said so before.

I noted in passing that the torches were placed seventeen feet apart.

Morrolan opened a door, behind which was a tight spiral staircase made of iron. I followed him up into a yet wider hall that seemed to slope upward, and that held more lamps and more ornate doorways. The walls were still black.

At one point I said, "There was no better way of getting me here?"

He said, "We could have kidnaped you."

He stopped before a large wooden door, upon which a crouching dzur was pictured. Morrolan pushed the door and it swung open.

The room was thirty feet on a side. Candles and torches provided the light. The chairs looked comfortable. All done in black. I've stated my opinion on that. Shadows flickered back and forth, making it hard to pick out objects . . .

. . . Someone was in one of the chairs. I took a wild guess as to who she might be. I stared at her. No one moved. She was gaunt, with a smooth, ageless aquiline face with hollowed-out cheeks, framed by straight hair that was black black black. Gods, but I was growing tired of black.

Perhaps she would have looked appealing to a Dragaeran, I don't know. She was very pale; in fact, it was startling that I hadn't seen her at once, there was such a contrast between her face and her surroundings. She wore black as well, of course. Her gown had high lace ruffles, coming to her chin. Below it, at her breast, was a large ruby. Her hands were long, and seemed even longer since her nails were done to a point. On the middle finger of her left hand was a ring that held what I think was a very large emerald. She stared at me with eyes that were deep and bright and old.

She stood up, and I saw that there was one splash of blue at her side, which I recognized as a jewel on the hilt of a dagger. Then I felt the dagger and knew it for at least as powerful a weapon as Morrolan's sword. As she stood, it vanished in a swirl of her cloak, which made her disappear entirely except for the dead white of her face, with those eyes gleaming at me like a wolf's.

I guess she'd decided to make me feel at home, because as she stood there the room brightened. That was when I saw, on the floor in front of me, face up, the lifeless body of Quion. His throat had been cut and the red of his blood was almost invisible against the black carpet.

"Welcome," she said in a voice that rolled from her tongue, as smooth as glass and as soft as satin. "I am Sethra."

No shit.

Among the customs peculiar to Easterners is the one involving the anniversary of one's birth. To the Easterners, this is a day for the person born to celebrate, rather than for him to honor and thank those who brought him into the world.

I spent my tenth birthday with my grandfather, mostly watching him work and enjoying it. I asked him questions whenever there wasn't a customer in the place, and learned about the three types of love potions, which herbs the witch should grow himself instead of buying, which incense should be used for which sorts of spells, why to make certain there are no mirrors or reflective surfaces nearby when doing magic, how to ensure an easy labor, cure cramps and headaches, prevent infection, and where to find spell books along with some idea of how to tell worthwhile spells from nonsense.

When he closed up shop, he said, "Come on back, Vladimir. Sit down." I went into his living area and sat in a big comfortable chair. He pulled up another chair and sat facing me. His cat, Ambrus, jumped onto his shoulder. I could hear it purring.

"Look at me, Vladimir." I did, wondering. He said, "Sink back into the chair now. Pretend you grow heavy, yes? Feel that you are getting heavy, and joining with the chair now. Can you do this? Keep looking at my face now, Vladimir. Think of me. Close your eyes. Try to still see me, even though your eyes are not open. Can you do this? Can you feel warm, now? Don't speak yet. Feel that you float in water, and you are warm. Think of my voice, see how it fills your head? Listen to how my voice rings in your head. Listen to nothing else. My voice is everything, all you know. Now, tell me this: How old are you?"

That puzzled me a little; I mean, did he think I'd fallen asleep, or what? I tried to answer him and was surprised at the effort it took. But I finally said, "Ten," and my eyes snapped open. My grandfather was smiling. He didn't say anything, because he didn't have to. As I'd said it, I had realized that the word "ten" had been the first word actually spoken aloud in the room for some few moments.

I stepped over the body as carefully as I could because it would have been embarrassing to slip. The Dark Lady of Dzur Mountain indicated a chair for me. I sat in another one only partly to be contrary—the one I chose wasn't as soft, and thus easier to get out of quickly. In case you haven't figured it out yet, I was, like, scared.

And I'll tell you another thing that surprised me: I felt bad about Quion. Sure, I'd been planning to kill him as soon as I caught up with him, but seeing him lying there dead like that, I don't know . . . I remembered how he'd been when he'd pleaded with me to let him work, and how he'd stopped gambling and all that, and it didn't seem as important that he'd stabbed me in the back by running off with my money. I suppose the fact that Morrolan had set him up for it made some difference.

But yeah, I was scared; I was also mad as a dzur in a chreotha net.

The Lord Morrolan sat facing me, working his chin and jaw. When I do that it means I'm nervous. I was inclined to think it meant something else in Morrolan, but I couldn't say what. A servant came in, dressed in black livery with a dragon's head on the left breast. I wondered what sort of man would be a servant to Sethra Lavode. From the roundness of his eyes and fullness of his face, I would have guessed him to be a Tsalmoth. He walked with his face cast down and his eyes squinting out from beneath tufts of hair sticking out from his brows. He seemed old. His tongue kept flicking out of his mouth, and I wondered if he were of sound mind. There was just the slightest bend to his waist. His walk was mostly a shuffle.

He presented us with aperitif glasses half filled with something the color of maple floors. He somehow managed to step over the body without appearing to notice it. He served me first, then Morrolan, then Sethra. His hands were splotched with white and shook with age. After serving us, still holding the tray, he stood behind Sethra and to her left, his eyes flicking around the room, never resting. His shoulders seemed permanently hunched. I wondered if he coordinated his eye motions with his tongue, but I didn't take the time to check. The drink turned out to be a liqueur that was sweet and tasted just a little like fresh mint.

I didn't want to stare at Sethra or Morrolan, so I found myself staring at Quion's body. I don't know about you, but I'm not used to having a quiet, social drink with a corpse on the floor. I wasn't sure what appropriate behavior was. After a couple of sips, however, I was relieved of the worry by Sethra taking charge. She whispered to the servant and put a purse on his tray. He shuffled over and, making eye contact with everything in the room except my face, delivered the purse to me.

Sethra Lavode said, "We had cause to borrow some of your funds."

How nice.

I chewed on the inside of my lip and tried to think about things that would distract me before I lost my temper completely and got myself killed. I hefted the bag while the servant bowed and returned to his place behind Sethra. On reflection, I decided that the hunching of his shoulders occurred when he stopped; rather like a runner sets himself to spring off the starting line. I signaled to him. He hesitated, glanced at his mistress, blinked about twelve times, and returned to me.

"Hold out the tray," I told him. He did, still not looking at me, and I slowly counted out fifteen hundred gold imperials in fifties and tens. "Give this to the Lady," I said. His mouth worked for just an instant, as if he had to think about it, and I noticed that he was missing some teeth. But then he brought the tray over to her. The entire scenario felt like a poorly blocked play.

Sethra stared at me. I held her gaze. She said, "This is . . . ?"

"Standard rates for the job you did," I explained, glancing at the body. "You do good—"

At which point the tray with the money went flying as Sethra Lavode struck it. She stood and her hand went to the hilt of her weapon. Morrolan also stood, and I swear he *growled*. I widened my eyes and did my innocent inquiring act, though my pulse was racing from that delicious mix of anger and fear that usually means someone is about to become damaged.

But Sethra stopped and raised her hand, which stopped Morrolan. Some portion of a smile came to Sethra's lips and she barely nodded. She sat down and looked a look at Morrolan. He also sat down, giving me a glare that said

"That's another one." The servant went about methodically picking up the gold and putting it back on the tray. It took him quite a while. I hoped he'd be able to palm some of it.

Sethra said, "All right, Jhereg. You've made your point. Can we get down to business now?"

Business. Right.

I cleared my throat. I said, "You wanted to talk business. You want to buy a title in the Jhereg? Sure, I can set that up. Or maybe you want to buy into—"

"Enough," said Morrolan.

I'll admit it: Push me far enough and anger overcomes self-preservation. I said, "Shove it, Dragonlord. I don't know what 'business' you think you have with me, but you have interfered with my work, murdered my employee, tricked me, and threatened me. Now you want to talk business? Shit. Talk away." I sat back, crossed my legs, and folded my arms.

They exchanged glances for a moment. Perhaps they were communicating psionically, perhaps only by expression. After a minute or so I sipped some more liqueur. The servant finished gathering the spilled money onto the tray. He started to offer it to Sethra again, but she glared at him. He gave some sort of grimace of resignation and set it down on a nearby table.

Sethra turned to me and said, "I don't know what to say. We thought you'd be pleased that we had killed this man and saved you the trouble—"

"Saved me the trouble? Who says I was going to kill him?" Well, sure, I was, but I wasn't going to admit to these two, was I? "And I wouldn't have needed to find him if you two hadn't—"

"Lord Taltos, please," said Sethra. She seemed genuinely contrite, and I guess the shock of that realization stopped me as much as her words. She said, "I assure you that all we did was help him choose the time for his theft. Morrolan's spell wouldn't have worked if he hadn't been planning to steal from you anyway." She paused, glanced at Morrolan, and shrugged. "We knew you to be a Jhereg as well as an Easterner, and had been expecting you to respond as a Jhereg only. Most of those in your House would have been happy to discuss a business deal no matter how they were brought into it. It seems we don't know Easterners. We have erred. We are sorry."

I bit my lip and thought about it. I would have felt better if Morrolan had expressed an apology, but there's something to be said for extracting one from the Enchantress of Dzur Mountain, isn't there? All right, I'll be honest. I still don't know if she was making all that up as she went along or if she was telling the truth, but believing her salved my pride a little. It allowed me to continue talking to them, at any rate.

I said, "Would you mind explaining to me why you went through all this in the first place?"

Sethra said, "Very well, then. Tell me this: Can you think of any other way we could have gotten you here?"

"Paying me would have worked."

"Would it have?"

I reflected. No, I suppose if they'd offered me enough to convince me to come, it would have just made me suspicious. I said, "If you'd wanted to see me, you could have come to me," I smirked. "The door to my office—"

"It is impossible for me to leave Dzur Mountain at the moment."

I gestured toward Morrolan. "And him?"

"I wanted to see you myself." She smiled a little. "Which is just as well, since I might have had some trouble convincing him to walk into a Jhereg's place of business."

Morrolan snorted. I said, "All right, I'm convinced that you're clever." I fell silent, but they seemed to be waiting for me to continue. What was there to say? I felt my jaw clenching with anger that hadn't yet died down. But, as I said, my best chance of getting out of there alive was cooperation. If they wanted me for something, they at least weren't going to kill me out of hand. I let out my breath and said, "Business, then. You have business in mind. Tell me about it."

"Yes." She sent Morrolan a glance that was impossible to read, then turned back to me. "There is a thing we'd like you to do."

I waited.

She said, "This is going to take some explanation."

• • •

During my entire tenth year it was almost impossible to keep me away from my grandfather's. I felt my father's growing dislike of this, and ignored it. Noish-pa was delighted at my interest in witchcraft. He taught me to draw things that I only saw in his mind, and gave me tours of his memories of his homeland. I still remember how it felt to see clear blue sky, with white puffy clouds and a sun so bright I couldn't look directly at it, even through the eyes of his memory. And I remember the stars as vividly as if I were there. And the mountains, and the rivers.

Finally my father, in an effort to distract me, hired a sorcerer to teach me. He was a snide young Jhegaala whom I hated and who didn't like me, but he taught me anyway and I learned anyway. I hate to think of what that cost my father. It was interesting, and I did learn something, but I resented it, so I didn't work as hard as I could have. In fact, I think I was working not to like it. But, on the other hand, I enjoyed the closeness with my grandfather much more than I enjoyed making pretty flashing lights in the palm of my hand.

This process continued for quite some time—until my father died, in fact. My grandfather had started teaching me fencing, in the one-handed, side-stance Eastern rapier style. When my father learned of it, he hired a Dragaeran sword teacher to show me the full-forward cut and slash sword and dagger method, which turned out to be a fiasco since I hadn't the strength to use even the practice sword of the Dragaerans.

The funny thing is, I suspect that if my father had ever actually told Noish-pa to stop, he would have. But my father never did; he only glowered and sometimes complained. I think he was so convinced that everything Dragaeran was better than everything Eastern, he expected me to be convinced of it, too.

Poor fool.

Sethra Lavode studied the floor, and the expression on her face was the one I wear when I'm trying to figure out a delicate way to say something. Then she nodded, almost imperceptibly, and looked up. "Do you know the difference between a wizard and a sorcerer?"

I said, "I think so."

"There aren't many who can achieve the skill in sorcery, necromancy, and other disciplines to combine them effectively. Most wizards are of the House of the Athyra or the House of the Dzur. Loraan is an Athyra."

"What was the name?"

"Loraan."

"I've never heard of him."

"No. You wouldn't have. He's never done anything remarkable, really. He is a researcher of magic, as are most Athyra wizards. If it means anything to you, he discovered the means by which the last thoughts of the dying may be preserved temporarily in fluids. He was attempting to find more reliable means of communicating with the dead by introducing a means of . . . "

After a few minutes of getting lost in a description of strange sorcery that I'll never need to know, I interrupted. "Fine," I said. "Let's just say he's good at what he does. What do you want from me?"

She smiled a little. Her lips were very thin and pale. She said, "He has in his possession a certain staff or wand, containing a necromantic oddity—the soul of a being who is neither alive nor dead, unable to reach the Plane of Waiting Souls, unable to reach the Paths of the Dead, unable to—"

"Fine," I said. "A staff with a soul in it. Go on."

Morrolan shifted and I saw his jaw working. He was staring at me hard but I guess exercising restraint. It occurred to me for the first time that they wanted me pretty badly.

Sethra said, "We have spoken to him at great length, but he is determined to keep this soul imprisoned. The soul is a wealth of information for him, and his work is all he cares about. He happened to acquire it shortly after the end of the Interregnum, and has no interest in giving it up. We have been trying to convince him to sell or trade it for several weeks now, ever since we discovered where it was. We have been looking for it for more than two hundred years."

I began to get the picture, and I didn't like it at all. But I said, "Okay, go on. How do I fit in?"

"We want you to break into his keep and steal the staff."

I said, "I'm trying to find a polite way of saying 'drop dead,' and not having much luck."

"Don't bother being polite," said Sethra with a smile that sent chills up and down my spine. "I died before the Interregnum. Will you take the job?"

4

I took hold of the knife I'd carried for so long and used so seldom. The one with the ebony hilt and embedded rubies, and the thin, dull blade of pure silver. It wasn't as expensive as it looked, but then, it looked very expensive.

I held it near the point, holding it firmly between my thumb and forefinger, then I knelt down, so slowly I felt tremors in my legs. Just as slowly, I touched the point of the dagger to the ground. I stopped for a moment, studying the dirt. It was black and dry and fine, and I wondered why I hadn't noticed it before. I touched it with my left hand. I rubbed it between my fingers. It was powdered and very cold.

Enough. I concentrated on the knife again, and very slowly drew the rune for the verb "to receive." The rune, of course, was in the language of sorcery, which was meaningless at this time and in this place. But it gave me a spot to concentrate my attention on, and that was what I wanted. I drew a circle around the rune then, and set the knife aside. I knelt and studied the drawing, waiting for the moment to begin again.

I was very much aware of Loiosh, claws hard on my right shoulder, a pressure more than a weight. It was as if none *of the events of the last few days had affected him, which I knew wasn't the case; he was the wall of calm, the pillar of ice, the ground that would hold me steady. If you think that isn't important, you're a bigger fool than I am.*

Moments went by in contemplation, and I began the next step.

There were no windows in the room, yet we must have been near the outside, because I could hear distant cries of ravens, and the occasional roar of a hunting dzur. I wondered if there were dragons on the mountain, present company excepted, of course. Why have a room with a wall to the outside and not put a window in it? Who knows? I like windows, but maybe Sethra Lavode doesn't. It is true that windows enable others to see in as well as allow you to see out.

A candle flickered and shadows danced.

"All right," I said. "Let's back up a little. If you want this staff so badly, why don't you and the Lord Morrolan here just blast into his keep and take it?"

"We'd like to," said Morrolan.

Sethra Lavode nodded. "One doesn't just 'blast into' the keep of an Athyra wizard. Perhaps if I were able to leave — but never mind."

I said, "Okay, fine. But look: I don't know what you know about me or what you think you know about me, but I'm not a thief. I don't know anything about breaking into places and stealing things. I don't know what made you think I could do it in the first place—"

"We know a great deal about you," said the Enchantress.

I licked my lips. "All right, then you know I'm not—"

"Close enough," said Morrolan.

"The point is," said Sethra Lavode before I could respond, "the particular nature of Loraan's alarm system."

"Ummmm, all right," I said. "Tell me about it."

"He has spells over the entire keep that keep track of every human being in the place, so any intruder, no matter how good, will be instantly detected. Neither Morrolan nor I have the skill to disable these alarms."

I laughed shortly. "And you think I do?"

"You weren't listening," said Morrolan. "His spells detect human beings—not Easterners."

"Oh," I said. Then, "Are you sure?"

"Yes," said Sethra. "And we also know that he has sufficient confidence in these alarms that he has little else that could detect you."

I said, "Do you know what the place looks like on the inside?"

"No. But I'm sure you have the resources—"

"Yeah, maybe."

Sethra continued. "Morrolan will be ready to aid you once you are inside."

A voice inside my head pointed out that Sethra appeared to be assuming I was going to do this crazy thing, and that she might be irritated when she learned I wanted no part of it. But I was curious; perhaps fascinated would be a better word.

Morrolan said, "Well?"

I said, "Well what?"

"Will you do it?"

I shook my head. "Sorry. I'm not a thief. As I said, I'd just bungle it."

"You could manage," said Morrolan.

"Sure."

"You are an Easterner."

I paused to look over my body, feet, and hands. "No. Really? Gosh."

Sethra Lavode said, "The individual whose soul lives in that staff is a friend of ours."

"That's fine," I said. "But it doesn't—"

"Seven thousand gold imperials," she said.

"Oh," I said after a moment. "A *good* friend of yours, eh?"

Her smile met my own.

"In advance," I said.

My grandfather is religious, though he never pressed the issue. My father rejected the Eastern gods as he rejected everything else Eastern. Naturally, then, I spent a great deal of time asking my grandfather about the Eastern gods.

"But Noish-pa, some Dragaerans also worship Verra."

"Don't call her that, Vladimir. She should be called the Demon Goddess."

"Why?"

"If you speak her name, she may become offended."

"She doesn't get angry at the Dragaerans."

"We aren't elfs. They don't worship as we do. Many of them know of her, but think she is only a person with skills and power. They do not understand the concept of a goddess the way we do."

"What if they're right and we're wrong?"

"Vladimir, it isn't a right and a wrong. It is a difference between those of our blood and those of the blood of Faerie— and those of the blood of gods."

I thought about that, but couldn't make it make sense. I said, "But what is she like?"

"She is changeable in her moods, but responds to loyalty. She may protect you when you are in danger."

"Is she like Barlan?"

"No, Barlan is her opposite in all ways."

"But they are lovers."

"Who told you that?"

"Some Dragaerans."

"Well, perhaps it is true, but it is not my concern or yours."

"Why do you worship Ver— the Demon Goddess and not Barlan?"

"Because she is the patron of our land."

"Is it true that she likes blood sacrifice? The Dragaerans told me that."

He didn't answer for a moment, then he said, "There are other ways to worship her and to attract her attention. In our family, we do not commit blood sacrifice. Do you understand this?"

"Yes, Noish-pa."

"You will never sacrifice a soul to her, or to any other god."

"All right, Noish-pa. I promise."

"You swear on this, on your powers as a witch and on your blood as my grandson?"

"Yes, Noish-pa. I swear."

"Good, Vladimir."

"But why?"

He shook his head. "Someday you will understand."

That was one of the few things about which my grandfather was wrong; I never have understood.

The teleport back to my office was no more fun than any of the others. It was early evening, and the shereba game in the room between the fake storefront and real office was in full swing. Melestav had left, so I thought the office was empty until I noticed Kragar sitting behind Melestav's desk. Loiosh flew onto my shoulder and rubbed his head against my ear.

"You okay, boss?"

"Well . . . "

"What is it?"

"It's hard to explain, Loiosh. Want to become a thief?"

"How'd it go, Vlad?"

"The good news is that no one hurt me."

"And?"

"And Sethra Lavode is certainly real."

He stared at me but said nothing.

"Well, what happened, boss?"

"I'll get to it, Loiosh."

"Kragar," I said, "this is going to get complicated." I paused and considered. "All right, sit back and relax; I'll tell you about it."

It would be nice if I could identify the point when I stopped fearing Dragaerans and started fighting back, but I can't. It certainly was before my father died, and that happened when I was fourteen. He'd been wasting away for quite a while, so it was no surprise, and, in fact, it didn't really bother me. He'd picked up some sort of disease and wouldn't let my grandfather perform the cures, because that was witchcraft and he wanted to be Dragaeran. He'd bought a title in the Jhereg, hadn't he?

Crap.

Anyway, I can't really pinpoint when I started hating Dragaerans more than I feared them, but I do remember one time—I think I was twelve or thirteen—when I was walking around with a lepip concealed in my pants. Lepip? It's a hard stick or piece of metal covered with leather. The leather keeps it from cutting; it's for those occasions when you don't want to leave scars, you just want to hurt someone. I could have used a rapier effectively, but my grandfather insisted that I not carry it. He said it was asking for trouble, and that drawing it would signal a fight to the death when otherwise someone would only be hurt. He seemed to feel that life should never be taken unless necessary, not even that of an animal.

In any case, I remember that on this occasion I deliberately walked through some areas where toughs of the House of the Orca liked to hang out, and yeah, they started harassing me, and, yeah, I creamed them. I think they just didn't expect an Easterner to fight back, and a heavy stick can make a big difference in a fight.

But that wasn't the first time, so I don't know. What's the difference, anyway?

I leaned back in my chair and said, "Kragar, I have another research project for you."

He rolled his eyes skyward. "Great. Now what?"

"There is a wizard named Loraan, of the House of the Athyra."

"Never heard of him."

"Get busy then. I need a complete drawing of his keep, including a floor plan, and a guess as to where he'd do his work."

"Floor plan? Of an Athyra wizard's keep? How am I supposed to get that?"

"You never let me in on your methods, Kragar; how should I know?"

"Vlad, why is it that whenever you get greedy, I have to risk my hide?"

"Because, in this case, you get ten percent."

"Of what?"

"Lots and lots."

"Say, that's even more than 'quite a bit,' isn't it?"

"Don't be flippant."

"Who, me? Okay, when do you want it? And if you say 'yesterday,' I'll—"

"Yesterday."

"—have to hurry. Spending limit?"

"None."

"I thought it might be one of those. I'll get back to you."

I don't really know when I killed a Dragaeran for the first time. When I'd fight them I was pretty casual about where and how hard I'd hit them, and I know that, more than once, there would be one or two of them stretched out on the ground when we were done. Thinking back on times I'd crack them on the top of the head with my lepip, I'd be surprised if none of them died. But I never found out for sure.

Every once in a while that bothers me. I mean, there's something frightening, in retrospect, in not knowing whether you killed someone. I think of some of those fights, and I remember most of them quite clearly, and I wonder where those people are today, if anywhere. I don't spend a lot of time wondering, though. What the hell.

The first time I knew that I had killed someone was when I was thirteen years old.

There is an interesting story in how Kragar managed to get the information I wanted, but I'll leave it to him to tell. He has peculiar friends. In the two days it took, I finished closing a deal on a gambling operation I'd been hungry for, convinced someone who owed money to a friend of mine that paying it was the gentlemanly thing to do, and turned down a lucrative proposal that would have taken three weeks and a Morganti dagger.

I hate Morganti weapons.

When Kragar returned with the drawings we spent a whole day going over them and coming up with stupid ideas. We were flatly unable to think up an intelligent one. We put the whole thing off for a day and tried again with the same results. Finally Kragar said, "Look, boss, the idea of breaking into an Athyra's keep is stupid. Naturally, any idea for how to do it is also going to be stupid."

I said, "Ummm, yeah."

"So just close your eyes and pick one."

"Right," I said.

And that's pretty much what I did.

We spent a few hours polishing it down to the point of least possible idiocy. When Kragar went off to make some of the arrangements, I closed my eyes and thought about Sethra Lavode. I called up a picture of her face, tried to "hear" her voice, and sent my mind out, questing. Sethra Lavode? Where are you, Sethra? Hello? Vlad, here . . .

Contact came remarkably easily.

She said, *"Who is it?"*

"Vlad Taltos."

"Ah. What do you want?"

"I have a plan for getting in. I need to make arrangements with you and Morrolan for timing and backup and stuff like that."

"Very well," she said.

It took about an hour, at the end of which I was no more confident than I'd been before speaking with her. But there you are. Orders went out, arrangements were made, and I reviewed my will. The stuff of life.

5 —

I felt very close to Loiosh, in tune with him. I discovered I was sitting cross-legged before the sorcery rune I'd drawn. I still had no idea why I'd drawn it in the first place, but it felt right.

It was quiet here. The wind, though almost still, whispered secret thoughts in my ear. I could clearly hear the rustle of fabric as Loiosh shifted slightly on my shoulder.

I began to feel something then—a rhythmic pulsing, disconcerting in that I was feeling it, not hearing it. I tried to identify its source, and could only conclude that it was coming from within me.

Strange.

I could try to ignore it, or I could try to understand it, or I could try to incorporate it. I opted for the latter and began to concentrate on it. A Dragaeran would have been impatient with its simplicity, but to me it was a rather attractive rhythm, soothing. My grandfather had told me that drums were often used in spells, back in his homeland. I could believe that. I allowed myself to fall into it, waiting until my skin seemed to vibrate in sympathy.

Then I reached out my right hand, slowly, gently, toward

the herbs and charms I'd laid out on that side. My hand touched something and I picked it up, brought it before my eyes without moving my head. It was a sprig of parsley. I set that in the center of the rune. I repeated the process with my left hand, and it brought back a clod of dirt from the Eastern home of my ancestors.

The dirt would reinforce arrival and safety; I had no idea what the parsley could represent in this context. I broke the dirt over the parsley. Behind the rune I placed a single white candle, which I also retrieved without looking. I kindled it, gently, with flint and a scrap of paper. A single candle burns brightly when it is the only source of light save the faint glow from the night sky.

It was then that I noticed the horizon before me, which had begun to flicker and waver, dancing, it seemed, in time to the pulsing of nonexistent drums. I decided not to let this disturb me unduly.

I contemplated my next action, waiting.

The very wealthy man drove his wagon up the hill toward the keep. This keep was actually a single, reddish stone structure, half of it underground, the other half in the form of a single tower.

It is a common misconception that those in the House of the Athyra have no doors into or out of their homes—the idea being that if one doesn't know how to teleport, one doesn't belong there. This is almost true, except that they don't require their servants to know how to teleport. There is almost always a door or two for deliveries of those goods the wizards and sorcerers of the keep consider too demeaning to fetch for themselves. Trivial things such as food, drink, and assassins. These items are delivered by wagons to a special receiving area in the rear, where they are received, each in its own way.

Of course, the assassins aren't usually expected and, one hopes, not noticed. Theirs is a sad lot, to be sure, with no servant within who knows to announce them. Nor, in fact, are they able to announce themselves, being hidden in a cask marked "Greenhills Wine, '637."

They are most certainly not going to be announced by

the very wealthy and equally terrified Teckla who delivers them and who, presumably, wishes to live to enjoy his newly acquired wealth.

No one was around to witness the various indignities I suffered during the unloading and storing process, so I shall refrain from mentioning them. It is sufficient to say that by the time I was able to break out of the stupid cask I was, fortunately, neither drunk nor drunk, if you take my meaning.

So . . . out. Stretch. Check my weapons. Stretch again. Look around. Do not make any rustling noises by getting out the floor plan, because you have it memorized. You *do* have it memorized, don't you? Think now—this is either *that* room or *that* room. Either way, the door lets out into a hall that leads . . . don't tell me now . . . oh, yes. Good. Shit. What, by all the gods of your ancestors, are you doing here, anyway?

Oh, yeah: money. Crap.

"You okay, boss?"

"I'll live, Loiosh. You?"

"I think I'll live."

"Good."

First step is getting the door open. Loraan may not be able to detect it when someone uses witchcraft within his keep, but I'm not going to bet *my* life on it; at least not unless I have to.

So I pulled a vial of oil from within my cloak, opened it, smeared its contents on the hinges, and tested the door. No, it wasn't locked, and yes, it opened silently. I put the oil away, sealing it carefully. Kiera had taught me that. This, you understand, is how assassins are able to sneak around so quietly: we cheat.

There was no light in the hall, and there shouldn't be any random boxes, either, according to Kragar's source. My favorite kind of door (an unlocked one) guarded the room where I chose to spend the remaining hours until the early morning hour I had selected. More oil, and I was inside. There was about a ten-to-one chance against anyone disturbing me in this room. If anyone did, Loiosh would wake me up and I'd kill the intruder. No sweat. Assuming no trouble,

Loiosh would keep track of time for me and wake me at the right hour. I spread out my cloak, closed my eyes, and rested. Eventually I slept.

The city of Adrilankha is most of County Whitecrest, which is a thin strip of land along the southern seacoast. The name "Adrilankha" means "bird of prey" in the secret language of the House of the Orca, which no one speaks anymore. The story is that the mariners who first sighted the area along the red cliffs thought it looked like such a bird, with bright red wings held high, head down at the sea level where the Sunset River cut through the land.

The low area around the river is where the docks were built, and the city grew up from it, until now most of the city is high above the docks and a long way inland. The two "wings" of the bird don't look much like wings anymore, since the northern wing, called Kieron's Watch, collapsed into the sea a few hundred years ago.

The southern wing has many good places from which to watch the waves crashing, and ships coming and going, and like that. I remember sitting there doing that sort of watching and not thinking about anything in particular when a Dragaeran—an Orca and probably a seaman—came staggering up next to me.

I turned and looked him over and decided he was drunk. He was pretty old, I think. At least, his face had turned into a prune, which doesn't usually happen to Orcas until they're at least a couple thousand years old.

As he came up, his eyes fell on me and I backed up a couple of steps from the cliff edge out of an instinctive mistrust of Dragaerans. He noticed this and laughed. "So, whiskers, you don't want to go swimming today?"

When I didn't say anything, he said, "Answer me. You want to go swimming or not?" I couldn't think of anything to say so I remained quiet, watching him. He snarled and said, "Maybe you ought to just leave, whiskers, before I send you for a swim whether you want one or not."

I don't know for sure why I didn't leave. Certainly I was frightened—this man was much older than the punks I usually had to deal with, and he looked tougher, too. But I just

stood there, watching him. He took a step toward me, perhaps just to frighten me away. I took my lepip from my
pants and held it at my side. He stared at it, then laughed.

"You think you're going to hit me with that, is that it?
Here, I'll show you how to use one of those things." And
he came at me with his hand out, to take it away.

What I remember most vividly is the cold thrill in my
stomach as I realized I wasn't going to let him take my
weapon. This wasn't a bunch of kids out to have a lark and
vent their frustration at whatever it was they were frustrated
about—this was a grown man. I knew I was committing myself to something that would have far-reaching effects,
though I couldn't have put it that way then.

Anyway, as soon as he was in reach I cracked him one
on the side of the head. He stumbled and fell to his knees.
He looked up at me, and I saw in his eyes that there wasn't
a beating at stake anymore; that he'd kill me if he had the
chance. He started to stand up and I went for him with the
lepip. I missed, but he fell over backward, rolled, and came
to his knees again.

His back was to the cliff, about two steps behind him.
The next time he tried to stand up, I stepped up and very
deliberately shoved him backward with the lepip.

He screamed all the way down, and I couldn't hear the
splash over the sound of the waves crashing against the cliff.

I put my lepip back in my pants and walked straight
home, wondering if I should be feeling something.

" . . . C'mon, boss, time to get up. There are six Dragon
warriors here, and they all want to duel with you. Let's go!
There's a Dzur hero knocking on the door asking about his
daughter, better get up. Okay boss, wake up! The Great
Sea of Chaos has just moved into the next bedroom and it
insists that you have a better view. Wakey wakey."

Waking up in the middle of the night, in a damp storage
closet, wedged between dried kethna ribs and a tub of lard,
with a wise-ass jhereg thundering smart remarks in your
mind, has little to recommend it.

"All right, stuff it, Loiosh."

I got up and stretched, worrying about the sound my

joints were making, though that was silly. I buckled on this
and checked that. I moved over to the door and spent a few
minutes listening to make sure there was no one out there.
I opened the door, which was still lubricated. Then left
down the hall, eighteen paces, oil the door, open it.

I was in the back of the kitchen. The morning cook
wouldn't be started for another couple of hours, and there
were no guards here. I moved across the kitchen and found
the door I wanted. Oil, open, walk. If the bastard had been
a little poorer, he would have had leather hinges on his
doors, which are easier to deal with. Or even empty doorways with curtains. Oil, open, walk. First checkpoint.

This door led down into the sublevels, and there were
a pair of Dragaeran guards here, in addition to sorcerous
alarms. The sorcery was simple and straightforward; mostly
token, and I had what the Left Hand of the Jhereg calls a
"device" and an Eastern witch would call a "charm" for
dealing with it. The guards would be more difficult. They
were more or less facing me and, unfortunately, awake.

I kill people for money; I don't like doing it when I don't
have to. But sometimes there just isn't any other way. I
studied the guards standing there and tried to think of a way
to avoid killing them.

I did not succeed.

Some time before this I had assassinated a certain money-
lender who, it turned out, had been skimming more than
his share out of the profits. His employer had been very
upset and wanted me to "make a 'xample outta the sonufa-
bitch." The boss arranged to meet the guy in a big, crowded
inn at the busiest time. The boss didn't show; instead, I
did. When my target sat down, I walked straight up to him,
put a dagger into his left eye, and walked out of the place.

One thing I remember about that is the wave of reaction
that followed me out the door, as the patrons of the inn
noticed the blood, the body, the event. None of them were
able to describe me, though many of them saw me.

What I'm getting at is the advantage of surprise—of the
attack that comes with no warning whatsoever. One moment
all is peaceful, the next there is an Easterner in your face,
knives flashing.

I hauled the bodies of the guards into the kitchen so they wouldn't be quite so obvious, then I picked the lock and headed down into the dungeon.

I guess it was my grandfather who really helped keep me going after my father died. It was funny how he did it. I mean, I've always hated being alone, but my grandfather felt that, at fourteen, I had to be independent, so he never responded to my hints that I could move in with him. Instead, he spent even more hours teaching me witchcraft and fencing, to give me something to do in my spare time.

It worked, too, in that I turned into a quite passable witch, a very good swordsman in the Eastern style, and that I learned to live alone.

I learned many things during that time, but it's taken the perspective of years to understand all of them. Like, I learned that to be not alone was going to take money. I had none, nor any means to acquire any (the restaurant I'd inherited from my father kept me alive and that was about it), but the lesson stuck with me, for the future.

I think practicing witchcraft was what did the most for me during that time. I could do things and *see* the results. Sometimes, in the peculiar trance state that witches fall into when performing, I'd see the entire thing as a metaphor of my life, and wonder if I'd ever be able to take control of my world and just *make* it be what I wanted.

Later, when I'd recovered from my attempt to take the salt out of seawater, or something equally useful, I'd take my lepip and go beat up a few Orca.

The other thing my grandfather did was insist—as did my father—that I have a good grounding in Dragaeran history. My grandfather found an Eastern tutor for me (he made me pay for it, too) who was quite good at those things, but who also knew something of the history of Fenario, the Eastern kingdom of my ancestors. I learned some of the language, too.

I would occasionally wonder what use these things would have for me, but then I'd start wondering about the rest of my life, and I just didn't want to think about that.

Oh, well.

• • •

So I went down. Real quiet, now. My eyes were already adjusted to the dark and there was a dim light from below; I was able to move quickly. The steps were narrow and deep, but solid stone. There was no railing. I concentrated on silence.

I reviewed The Plan: get down to the level where Loraan would—I hope—keep such things as souls contained in staffs, unlock the door (breaking any spells necessary without alerting Loraan), and have Morrolan launch his surprise (we hoped) attack on the keep's defenses just hard enough and long enough to teleport us both out of there.

It occurred to me again that I'd never before depended on any form of magic to get me out of something. I didn't like it. I reviewed the various ways I could ditch and run at this point, which took no time at all.

Ah! The bottom!

There was one guard here. Unlike the two upstairs, he was dozing, which saved his life. I made sure he wouldn't wake any time soon, and continued. Left for twenty-five paces, and to a door. This one was big and strong, and the lock, I'd been told, was serious. I studied it, and it was. But then I'm pretty good.

My fingers twitched as I studied the dead-bolt and the hinges. Frankly, though, I was more worried about the spells that sealed it, as well as any that might trigger alarms. I estimated the door itself to weigh about forty pounds. It was composed of thick wooden planks with iron bands around them. It wasn't perfectly sealed, though, since light was coming from the other side of it. I didn't know what that meant; this was where my information ended. I licked my lips and started working.

Kiera the Thief had not only found a set of burglar tools for me, but had trained me in their use. I'm not a thief, but I get by. I hoped the "device" was up to overcoming the alarms, because I wasn't; defeating the lock was the most I could hope for.

A good lock combines a fine mechanism with a heavy bolt. This one had, indeed, a very fine mechanism, and three separate dead-bolts. So the pick had to be strong enough to turn the bolts, but light enough to go into the lock. It turned out to be a three-tumbler system, requiring a spring-pick and three rods, all of which had to be pressed against tumblers going in different directions while being turned in yet a fourth direction. If my fingers had been much smaller and I'd had an extra pair of arms, it would have been much easier. As it was, it took me twenty minutes, but I got it, and no alarms went off as far as I could tell.

I would have forgotten to oil the hinges but Loiosh reminded me. On the other side was a landing with several lamps blazing and stairs leading down to a set of three doors, all of which looked—from up here—to be rather flimsy.

I spent about fifteen minutes locking the heavy door again. This may have been a waste of time; I couldn't decide. Then I took a couple of deep, silent breaths, closed my eyes, and—

"What is it, Vlad?" One is always on a first-name basis in psionic communication, because magic transcends courtesy.

"I'm past the big door."

"All right. I'll inform Morrolan. We'll stay in contact. As soon as you have the staff in your hand, we'll break the teleport block. It won't be down for long."

"So you've said."

"And I repeat it. Be careful."

"Yeah."

Once at the bottom, I had to pick a door. None of them were locked or enchanted, so I chose the middle one. I oiled the hinge and slipped it open. Forty-five minutes later I was back in front of the three doors, and I had a much better idea of the sorts of seashells Loraan liked to collect, and a very good idea of his taste in art, but no better idea of where the staff was.

I wondered how long it would be until someone discovered the bodies in the kitchen, or noticed that the guards weren't at their posts.

I really hated this. I tried the left-hand door.

The room was lit, though I couldn't see the light source. It was about forty paces square, with another door opposite me. A large table, say ten feet long, dominated the middle of the room. There were globes suspended from the ceiling, emitting narrow beams of light that were concentrated on a single point at one side, and near this point was a stack of thick, heavy tomes. There was another tome on the table, open, with a quill pen next to it and half a page written in. Small, glittering stones were scattered on the table. Three wands—none of which matched the description of what I was looking for—stood against the wall to my left, and a pedestal at the end of the table held what seemed to be a chain made of gold, suspended in air except for the end that touched the pedestal. A broadsword leaned against the table, and it would have looked incongruous save that from where I stood I could see that it was covered with runes and symbols. Against another wall was a large basin, probably holding something unnatural to which unmentionable things had been done.

In case you haven't figured it out yet, this was Loraan's work area.

I studied the floor in front of me for a long time, checking the path to the door opposite. It seemed to be clear. I let my observations flow back to Sethra. She acknowledged but didn't comment. I crossed very carefully and reached the other door without making a sound.

I studied this door for quite a while. No spells, no bolts, no alarms. I oiled the hinges just to be safe, then opened it. I was in a slightly smaller room, not as cluttered. The only thing of note was what seemed to be a cube made of orange light, about six feet on a side, in the middle of the room. In the center of the glowing cube was a white, five-foot-long staff. At one end I could almost make out the rusty star I'd been told to look for.

That was not, however, the only thing in the room.

Next to the cube of light, facing it, was a Dragaeran. He stared at me and I stared at him. He is frozen that way in my mind—all of seven and a half feet tall, big, thick eyebrows on a florid face, with long, tangled reddish hair that stuck out at improbable angles. He was old, I guess, but he certainly wasn't infirm. He stood straight, and his stance reminded me of Morrolan just before he had almost attacked me. I saw the lines of muscles beneath his tight, white blouse, and the blood-red cloak he wore was drawn back, held by a ruby clasp that reminded me of Sethra's. His brown eyes were clear and unblinking, yet his expression seemed mildly curious, neither frightened nor angry.

Only his hands seemed old — long fingers that were twisted and bent, with what might have been tiny scars all over the backs of his fingers. I have no idea what could have caused that. In his hands was a dark, thin tube, about four feet long, that was pointed at the staff inside the orange cube.

The bastard was working late tonight.

I would almost certainly have beaten him to the draw, as it were, if he hadn't noticed me coming in. He gestured vaguely in my direction and I discovered I couldn't move. A black fog swam before my eyes. I said, "*Sorry, Sethra, not this time.*" And nothing held me as I sagged against nothing, fell in, and was buried.

6 ▫

I stared at the flickering, weaving dance of the horizon and tried to decide if I liked it, or if it mattered. The thought that I was losing my mind came, and I pushed it aside. It is a not uncommon fear in such circumstances, largely because it sometimes happens. But I just didn't have time to deal with it then.

My eyes were drawn from the wavering landscape to the sorcery rune I had, for whatever reason, drawn on the ground before me. I blinked and it didn't go away. I licked my lips.

The rune was glowing. I hadn't asked it to, but I guess I hadn't asked it not to, either.

I brought my palms together in front of me, fingers pointing out, and in the air I drew another rune, this one the verb "to summon." I considered what nouns I might hang from it, shuddered, and almost lost control of the spell. Loiosh pulled me back and I dropped my hands back to my lap.

The rhythm was still with me and the landscape still wavered and the rune on the ground still glowed.

I think the other sound was my teeth grinding.

• • •

I was unconscious for about twenty seconds, near as I can figure it. The side of my face still stung from slapping the floor, as did my right hand.

I awoke slowly, and swirls of black dissipated before me. I know better than to shake my head under such circumstances; my eyes cleared.

Loraan was leaning up against the far wall, staring past me, both his arms raised. I turned my head and saw Morrolan, who seemed to be fighting something invisible that was trying to entangle him. Sparks flashed in the air between them—that is, directly over my head.

I was being rescued. Oh, rapture.

I was about to try to convince my body to function—at least enough to get out from between the two of them—when Loraan gave a kind of cry, struck the wall behind him, bounced, and came careening at me. I would have put a knife into him then and there but he fell on top of me before I could go into action.

This is called "not being in top form."

Loraan was quite agile, though, especially for a wizard. After landing on me he kept rolling until he ended up in the room with Morrolan, as well as the table, the sword, the staves, and all that stuff. He came smoothly to his feet and faced Morrolan.

There was a bit of confused action lasting maybe ten seconds, including smoke and sparks and fire and loud noises, and when it was over Morrolan had his back to me and Loraan was too far away for any of my goodies to be effective.

Loiosh, who had been so quiet I'd all but forgotten him, said, *"Should we get the staff now?"*

Oh, yeah. Right. The staff. What we came for.

I got to my feet, a little surprised that they worked, and moved toward the cube of orange light. I began studying the enchantment on it and muttering curses to myself. I didn't know what it was or how it had been accomplished, but I could tell it wouldn't be safe to put my hand in there; I could also tell that breaking it would be *way* over my head. I wondered if Morrolan would be open to taking a job. I turned back to the fight to ask him.

I was almost sixteen when I decided I was old enough to ignore my grandfather's advice, and started carrying my rapier. It wasn't a very good one, but it had a point, an edge, and a guard.

I'd been carrying it for less than a week before I learned that my grandfather was right. I was heading back to the restaurant from the market at the time. On reflection, an Easterner with a sword at his hip carrying a basket full of fish, meat, and vegetables must have looked a bit absurd, but at the time I didn't think about that.

I heard laughter as I was near the door and saw two kids, roughly my age (taking different growth rates into account), dressed in the livery of the House of the Hawk. They were clearly laughing at me. I scowled at them.

One laughed harder and said, "Think you're pretty dangerous, don't you?" I noticed he was also wearing a blade.

I said, "Could be."

He said, "Want to show me how dangerous?"

I set the basket down and walked into the alley, turned, and drew, my pulse racing. The pair of them walked up to me and the one with the weapon shook his head in mock sadness. He was quite a bit taller than I, and may have had good reason to be confident.

He took his sword in his right hand and a long fighting knife in his left. I noted that he probably wasn't going to use sorcery, or his left-hand weapon would have been different. My grandfather's words came back to me, and I put a little more mental emphasis on the word "probably."

He faced me, full forward, both arms extended, right arm and right leg a bit more. I came into a guard position, presenting only my side, and a look of puzzlement came over his features.

I said, "Get on with it."

He took a step toward me and began an attack. At that time, I had no idea of just how much of an advantage in speed and technique there was to the Eastern style of fencing. I actually wondered why he was taking such big actions, and wondering prevented me from stop-cutting his exposed forearm. However, I still had time to shift backward, which I did, and his cut missed.

He came at me again, in the same slow, stupid way, and this time I did put a cut on his arm before pulling back out of the way. He made a sound of some sort and dropped his knife out of line.

His heart was wide open, with absolutely no protection. How could I resist? I nailed him. He gave out a yell, dropped both of his weapons, fell over backward, and began rolling on the ground. Before he hit the ground I was pointing my weapon at his companion, who was staring at me, wide-eyed.

I approached the uninjured one then and, as he stood there, cleaned my blade on his garments, still staring him in the eye. Then I sheathed my rapier and walked out of the alley, picked up my basket, and continued home.

On the way, I decided that my grandfather had certainly known what he was talking about: Wearing a weapon is asking for trouble.

I continued to wear it.

Everyone should, at least once, have the chance to witness a fight between two wizards. I'd have preferred to watch this one from more of a distance, though. The air between them seemed to dance, and my eyes had trouble focusing. Loraan held a staff with his right hand, in front of him. The tip of it was glowing with a sort of gold, and images behind the glow were blurred and out of focus. His other hand continually made motions in the air, and sometimes my ears would pop—from what I'm not sure.

I could see that Morrolan was hard-pressed. He had lost whatever advantage he had gained, and was leaning against a wall. There was a black mist in front of him, pushing against something invisible that was trying to get through to him. From thirty feet away I could make out the sweat on his forehead.

Loraan took a step forward. Morrolan raised his hands. The black mist in front of him grew thicker. I recalled an old maxim: Never attack a wizard in his keep. The black mist dissipated completely, and Morrolan seemed to shrink against the wall. Loraan took another step forward and raised his hands. I recalled another old maxim, this one concerning wizards and knives. Loraan's back was to me now, more or less.

My dagger caught him high on his back next to his backbone, though it didn't quite hit his spine. He stumbled. Morrolan straightened and took a step forward. He turned to Loraan. Loraan promptly vanished; one of the fastest teleports I've ever seen. Morrolan gestured at him as he was going, and there was a flash of bright light, but I didn't think it had accomplished anything. I entered the room and approached Morrolan.

He turned to me. "Thank you, Lord Taltos."

I shrugged. "I can't figure out how to get the staff out of whatever it is he's got in in."

"Okay. Let's—"

Clang. The door burst open and Dragaerans started pouring through. About a zillion of them, give or take a few. Most of them had the sharp chins and high foreheads of the House of the Dragon, though I thought I saw a Dzur or two. They all wore the red and white of the Athyra. I looked at their broadswords and longswords as I drew my cute little rapier. I sighed.

"No, Vlad," said Morrolan. "Get the staff. I'll hold them."

"But—"

Morrolan drew his sword, which assaulted my mind by its very presence, and the room seemed to darken. I'd known it was Morganti the first time I'd seen it, but he hadn't actually drawn it in my presence before. Now . . .

Now I suddenly knew it for a Great Weapon, one of the Seventeen. A blade that could break kingdoms. Its metal was as black as its pommel, and its heart was grey. It was small for a longsword, and it seemed to absorb the light from the room. The demons of a thousand years came and sat upon my shoulder, crying, "Run, as you value your soul."

Our eyes locked for a moment. "I'll hold them," he repeated.

I stood there, staring, for perhaps a second, then snapped back. "I can't get it out of—"

"Right," he said and glanced around the room. If you're

wondering about the guards during this whole exchange, they were stopped in the doorway, staring at Morrolan's sword and, I suppose, trying to work up courage to attack. Morrolan's eyes came to rest on the pedestal on which one end of the golden chain rested, the other end hanging, coiled, in midair.

"Try that," said Morrolan.

Right. Just the sort of thing I wanted to play with.

I raced over and, trying hard not to think, grabbed the end of the chain near where it touched the pedestal. It wasn't fastened, coming away easily in my hand, still coiling in midair like a snake about to strike. I crossed over to the door beyond which was the cell. I paused long enough to look at the tableau of guards and Morrolan. All of their eyes were riveted on that blade.

Perhaps their courage would have failed them and they wouldn't have attacked, I don't know. But while they were considering, Morrolan charged. One sweep of that blade and one fell, his body almost cut in half from right shoulder to left hip. Morrolan lunged and took the next through the heart and he screamed. A stream of what I can only describe as black fire came from Morrolan's left hand and more cries rose.

I turned away, not doubting that he could hold them off—as long as Loraan didn't show up again.

I hurried to the glowing cube.

The chain looked like it was made of gold links, each link about half an inch long, but as I held it, it seemed much harder than gold. I wished I'd had the time to study it, at least a little. I ran my left hand over it, in a kind of petting motion. It wasn't held in the air rigidly, so I pushed it down. There was a bit of resistance, then it hung free, like a chain is supposed to. I felt worlds better. I took a moment to reflect and to allow my life to pass before my eyes if it chose to (it didn't), and then, for lack of any other ideas, struck the chain against the orange glow, bracing myself to take whatever kind of backlash it generated. A light tingling ran up my arm. The glow became a flare and was gone.

A white staff with a rusty star at the end lay on the floor. I swallowed and picked it up. It felt a bit cold, and was perhaps heavier than it ought to have been, but nothing happened to me when I touched it. I turned, holding my trophies, toward the sounds of mayhem.

As I walked back into the room, I was nearly blinded by a flash of light. I managed to blink and duck my head enough to avoid most of it, so I was able to look up and see perhaps two dozen bodies lying on the floor. Morrolan was standing, feet braced, his sword acting as a shield to hold off a barrage of white light coming from—

Loraan!

I cursed softly to myself. He now held both a red staff and a small rod or wand. The light was coming from the staff, and, as I entered, I saw him look at me and look at the staff in my hand; his eyes grew wide. Then he saw the chain and they grew wider, and I even saw him mouthing a curse which I recognized and won't repeat. He turned the rod toward me. I fell over backward as a blue sheet of . . . something came rolling toward me. I might have screamed. I threw my hands up in front of my face.

The golden chain was still in my right hand. As I threw my hands up, it swung out in front of me and struck the sheet of blue, which promptly evaporated. All I felt was a tingling in my arm.

It's all in the wrist, see.

By this time I was flat on my back. I raised my head in time to see Morrolan step toward Loraan, stop, curse loudly, and begin to gesture with his left hand. Loraan was still looking at me, which I didn't like at all. Then he turned the staff so it was pointed at me, which I liked even less.

I felt as if I'd been kicked in the head and stomach at the same time, lying there on my back, waiting for him to do whatever it was he was going to do. Somehow he was holding off Morrolan, who would have killed him then if it were possible, so the wizard must have had some sort of sorcerous defense against physical attacks.

"Suggestions, Loiosh?"

"I'll bet he doesn't have any defense against witchcraft, boss."

"Sure. Now just give me an hour or two to set up a spell,

and—" No, wait. Maybe it wasn't such a bad idea after all. Witchcraft is controlled psychic energy. Maybe I could—

I sat up, setting the chain to spinning in front of me, hoping that would prevent whatever Loraan wanted to do to me. I saw him gnash his teeth and turn back and gesture with the rod at Morrolan, who gave a cry and fell against the far wall.

I allowed my psychic energy to flow into a dagger I pulled, and I think I chanted something, too. Then I let the chain fall and threw the dagger. Loraan waved his arms and something hit me and I fell backward, cracking my head against the floor. I wondered which one of us would get it. Maybe both.

I heard a scream from what seemed to be the right direction, and then Morrolan was hauling me up. I shied away from his sword, but he held me. My left hand still gripped the chain.

"Come on, dammit! Stand up. He summoned help, and I've been holding them off for the last minute. We have to get out of here."

I managed to support myself, and saw Loraan. My knife was in his stomach, and there was a large cut, as from a sword, in his chest, directly over the heart. He seemed to be rather dead. Morrolan was holding the white staff. Just about then figures began to appear all around us. Morrolan gestured with his free hand. The walls vanished.

We were lying on hard stone. I recognized the place where I had first arrived at Dzur Mountain. Morrolan collapsed onto the floor. The staff went rolling off to the side. I threw up.

7 -

I began to feel a slight giddiness, but that was to be expected, and I could ignore it if it didn't get any worse. I dropped my eyes from the empty spot in front of me and studied the glowing rune. If the rune was here, then the object of my desire was—there.

I touched the spot, making a small impression with my forefinger. I picked up one of the knives I'd laid out—the small, sharp one—and made a cut in the palm of my left hand. It stung. I held it over my right hand until I'd cupped a few drops of blood; then I let the blood dribble into the impression in the dirt. It was soaked up immediately, but that was all right.

I picked up the stiletto with my right hand, then wrapped my left hand around it, too. There would be blood on the handle, but that wouldn't hurt this; might even help. I raised the stiletto high and focused on the target. It was every bit as important to strike dead on as it was when striking at a person. This was easier, though, as I could take my time.

The moment was right; I plunged the weapon into the ground, the depression, the blood.

I saw, for just an instant, a sheet of white before my eyes,

*and my ears were filled with an incomprehensible roar, and
there was the smell of fresh parsley. Then it was all gone,
and I was left with the rhythm, the glowing rune, and the
queer landscape. And, in addition, a certain feeling of fulfillment.*

The link was forged.

I began composing my mind for the next step.

We made it back up to the library and found seats. I
closed my eyes and leaned back. Loiosh spent his time
hissing at Morrolan and being generally jumpy. I was feeling
a bit weak-kneed, but not too bad, all in all. Morrolan kept
glancing at Loiosh, as if he didn't quite know what to make
of him. I rather enjoyed that.

Sethra Lavode joined us. She nodded to each of us,
glanced at Loiosh without remarking on his presence, and
sat down. Her servant, whose name turned out to be Chaz,
came in and was sent out again. While he was getting refresh-
ments, Loiosh was staring at the Dark Lady of Dzur mountain.

"That's her, boss? Sethra Lavode?"

"Yeah. What do you think?"

"Boss, she's a vampire."

"I'd wondered about that. But is she a good vampire or
a—"

"Have we ever run into her before?"

"Ummm, Loiosh, I think we'd remember if we had."

"Yeah, I guess."

While this was going on, the lady under discussion held
out her hand toward Morrolan. He gave her the staff. She
studied it for a moment, then said, "Someone is, indeed,
inside of it." As she was saying it, Chaz walked back in.
He glanced quickly at the staff and went on with serving
us. Well, if he can step over bodies, he can ignore people
inside wizard staffs, I guess.

Morrolan said, "Is it she?"

"I will tell you anon."

She sat there for a moment longer, her eyes closed. At
one point Chaz stepped up behind her with a cloth and wiped
her forehead, which I hadn't noticed had become sweaty.

He still never looked up. Then Sethra announced, "It passes the tests. It is she."

"Good," said Morrolan.

"I will begin work on it then. Chaz, open up the west tower."

As the servant left, without answering or acknowledging, Morrolan said, "Shall I ask the Necromancer to come by?" I didn't know to whom Morrolan referred here, but I heard the capital letter.

"No," said the Enchantress. "Perhaps later, if there are problems."

Morrolan nodded and said, "How have things been here?"

"Difficult." I noticed then that she seemed a little harried and worn out, as if she'd just been through a rough experience of some kind. None of my business.

Her eyes fell on the chain I was still holding in my left hand. "Is that yours?"

I said, "Yes."

"Where did you find it?"

"An Athyra wizard gave it to me."

She maybe smiled a bit. "How kind of him." She stared at it for a moment longer, then said, "Have you named it?"

"Huh? No. Should I?"

"Probably."

"Care to tell me about it?"

"No."

"All right."

She took the staff and walked out of the room. I wrapped the chain around my left wrist and asked Morrolan if he'd be good enough to teleport me back to my home. He said he'd do this, and he did.

I'd first met Kiera when I was eleven years old, during an altercation in my father's restaurant, and she'd been inordinately kind to me—the first Dragaeran who ever was. We'd been in touch off and on since then. Once I asked her why she liked me, when every other Dragaeran I'd met hated me. She'd just smiled and tousled my hair. I didn't bother asking a second time, but I wondered quite a bit.

She wore the grey and black of the House into which my

father had purchased orders of nobility, but I eventually learned that she actually worked for the organization—that she was a thief. Far from being disturbed by this, I always found it fascinating. Kiera taught me a few things, too, like picking locks, disabling sorcery alarms, and moving through crowds without being noticed. She offered to teach me more, but I was just never able to picture myself as a thief.

I don't want to talk about all the boring business stuff associated with running a restaurant, but there was one time—I think I was fifteen—when it looked like I'd have to sell the place due to some weird tax thing. In the midst of trying to decide how to deal with this, the pressure let up, and the imperial tax man stopped coming around.

I've never been one to let well enough alone, so I started looking for him, to find out what was going on. Eventually I saw the guy harassing another merchant in the area and asked him about it.

"It's been taken care of," he said.

"How?"

"It was paid."

"Who paid it?"

"Didn't you?"

"Maybe."

"What do you mean, maybe?"

I thought fast. "I'm missing some money," I said, "and there was someone who should have taken care of it, and I just want to make sure it was done."

"A Jhereg paid it off. A lady."

"Wearing a grey cloak with a big hood? Long hands, a low voice?"

"Right."

"Okay, thanks."

A week or so later I noticed Kiera in an alley, leaning against a building. I walked up to her and said, "Thanks."

She spoke from out of her hood. "For what?"

"Paying off my taxes."

"Oh, that," she said. "You're welcome. I want you to owe me a favor."

I said, "I already owe you about a hundred. But if there's something I can do for you, I'd be happy to."

She hesitated, then said, "There is."

I got the vague impression that she was making this up as she went along, but I said, "Sure. What is it?"

She pushed the cowl back and stared at me. She chewed her lip, and it suddenly startled me that Dragaerans did that, too.

It always surprises me how young she seems, if you don't look into her eyes. She made a slow careful scan of the alley. When she turned back to me, she was holding something in her hand. I took it. It was a small, clear vial with a dark liquid inside; perhaps an ounce. She said, "Can you hold this for me? I don't think it will be dangerous to you. It *is* dangerous for me to hold it just now."

I studied the vial to see how breakable it was. It wasn't very. I said, "Sure. How long do you think you'll want me to hang on to it?"

"Not long. Twenty, thirty years maybe."

"Huh? Kiera—"

"Oh. Yes. I guess that is a long time to you. Well, perhaps it won't be that long. And, as I say, it shouldn't be dangerous for you."

She handed me a small pouch on a cord. I slipped the vial into it and put it around my neck.

I said, "What's in the vial?"

She paused, appearing to consider, then covered her head again. "The blood of a goddess," she said.

"Oh." And, "I don't think I'll ask."

I woke up the night after my altercation with Loraan feeling a peculiar half-thought growing in the back of my head and realized that someone was trying to reach me psionically. I woke up more fully, saw that it was almost dawn, and allowed the contact to occur.

"Who is it?"

"Sethra Lavode."

"Oh. Yes?"

"We need your help."

Several remarks came to mind, but I didn't make any of them. *"Go on,"* I said.

"We'd like to bring you here."

"When?"

"Right away."

"Mind if I break my fast first?"

"That will be fine. Would you like us to have a bucket ready for you to throw up in?"

Bitch. I sighed. *"All right. Give me ten minutes to wake up and become human."*

"What?"

"Become Eastern, then. Never mind. Just give me ten minutes."

"All right."

I rolled over and kissed Szandi's neck. She mumbled something incomprehensible. I said, "I have to run. Help yourself to breakfast and I'll see you later, okay?"

She mumbled again. I got up and took care of necessary things, including wrapping the gold chain around my left wrist and putting various weapons in place. Loiosh landed on my shoulder as I was finishing.

"What is it, boss?"

"Back to Dzur Mountain, chum. I don't know why."

I walked down to the street and around a corner and waited. Sethra reached me again right on time, and then I was at Dzur Mountain.

I wondered about the vial Kiera had given me, holding what she claimed to be the blood of a goddess. When I got back home, I took it out of its pouch and studied it. It was dark and could have been blood as easily as anything else, I suppose. I shook it, which was perhaps foolish but no harm came of it. Yeah, maybe it was blood. Then again, maybe not. I put the vial back in the pouch. I chose not to open it. I wondered if I would ever learn the story behind why Kiera had it but didn't want to hold onto it and couldn't sell it and like that. I realized that it made me feel good to do something for her for a change.

I put it in a chest where I kept my few precious objects and didn't think about it again for some time. I had other things to keep me occupied. My grandfather had decided that, as part of my ongoing training in witchcraft, it was time for me to acquire a familiar.

•   •   •

Ten minutes after I got there, I was deciding that I could come to like Sethra, after all. They brought me straight into the library this time, and, after giving me ten minutes to recover from the teleport, Chaz showed up with hot, good klava (klava is a strange Dragaeran brew made from Eastern coffee beans. It tastes like Eastern coffee but without the bitterness). She had thick cream and honey to put into it, and hot biscuits with butter and honey. Morrolan and I sat around eating and sipping for a good, long while. Chaz stood behind Sethra, occasionally eating bits of the crumbs off the tray and flicking his eyes around the room.

I studied Morrolan because he still fascinated me. He seemed to be working to keep any expression off his face, which probably meant that he was pretty concerned about something. I speculated idly but came up with no good guesses, so I concentrated on eating and drinking.

I have to say I was quite surprised by the food and even more surprised, and pleased, when the servant brought Loiosh a fresh dead teckla. He presented it to me and indicated Loiosh with a sort of half-flick of his head, as if he thought I might not know for whom it was intended. He set the tray down, and Loiosh started in on it, displaying his best table manners. Neither Sethra nor Morrolan seemed put off at eating with him.

"These people are okay, boss."

"I was just thinking that."

What shocked me even more, however, was the sight of Lord Morrolan, wizard and witch, duke of the House of the Dragon, licking honey off his fingers. It's a shame Dragaerans don't have facial hair, because Morrolan ought to have had a black goatee to get honey in.

If the whole thing was a scheme to put me in a better mood for helping them, I can only say it worked. I found it, at least, far preferable to the last idea they'd come up with. When the bowls of warm water with the steamed towels came around, I was pretty much willing to listen to any crazy idea they'd come up with.

It was plenty crazy, too.

•   •   •

The spell to acquire a familiar is as old as witchcraft, and has as many variations as there are types of familiars and families of witches. It is a simple spell by the standards I'm used to, but has some risks beyond those inherent in performing any ritual to which you are committing your mental energy. For instance, it meant wandering alone through the jungle. I'd asked my grandfather why I couldn't simply find one of the jhereg that fly about the city, and he asked me if I'd ever seen any of them close up.

My grandfather gave me a pack and stern lectures on what to put in it, and only general comments on hazards to avoid. I asked him why he couldn't be more specific, and he said it was because he didn't know. That scared me. I said, "Are you sure this is safe, Noish-pa?"

He said, "Of course not, Vladimir. I will tell you that it has much danger. Do you wish to not do it?"

"Ummm, no. I guess I'll go ahead with it."

Then I spent many hours in study of the wildlife of the jungles west of Adrilankha. I think my grandfather knew I'd do that, and, in fact, that was why he'd phrased things the way he did. I learned a great deal as a result. The most important thing was to study carefully anything that might hurt you.

This lesson has held me in very good stead.

"Wait a minute," I said. "Start over. Just exactly *why* am I supposed to pack up and trundle off to the Paths of the Dead?"

Remember how you felt the first time you buckled on a sword and went stomping around town? Remember the scabbard clanking against your leg? Remember touching the hilt with your off hand every now and then, just to reassure yourself it was there? If you've never done it, try to imagine the feeling. There's nothing quite like it; a little voice in the back of your head goes, "I'm dangerous now. I matter."

If you can remember that, or imagine it, think about how you'd feel the first time you slipped a dagger into your sleeve and another into your boot, and concealed a few shuriken in the folds of your cloak. All of a sudden you feel, I don't know, like a force to be reckoned with. Does that make sense?

Now, in point of fact, you don't want to show this at all. I never had to be told this; it's obvious. Even in subtle ways, you don't want to project the feeling of danger; you'd rather disappear. But there it is, anyway. Walking around with lethal surprises about your person changes the way you look at life; especially if you're a sixteen-year-old Easterner in a city of Dragaerans. It feels great.

Why was I walking around carrying concealed weaponry? Because I'd been advised to by someone who ought to know. She'd said, "If you're going to work for the Organization—and don't kid yourself, Vlad, that's what you're doing—it's always best to have a few surprises about you."

That's what I was doing: working for the Organization. I'd been given a job. It wasn't clear exactly what my job was, except that it could involve violence from time to time, starting with today. I was human, hence smaller and weaker than the Dragaerans I lived among. Yet I didn't fear violence from them, because I knew I could hurt them. I'd done so. More than once.

Now, for the first time, I was going to be paid for it, and I sure didn't mind. Whatever becomes of me, I'm going to hold the memory of walking from my tiny little flat to the shoemaker's where I was to meet my partner for the first time. A newly hatched jhereg whom I was going to make my familiar nestled against my chest, reptilian head lying just below my neck, wings tucked in, claws gripping the fabric of my jerkin. Occasionally I would "hear" him in my mind: *"Mama?"* I'd send back comforting thoughts that somehow didn't conflict with the rather violent frame of mind I was in.

It was the sort of day you look back on later and see as a pivotal point in your life. Thing is, I knew it at the time. It was a day when magic things were happening. Every time I swung my left arm, I'd feel the hilt of a dagger press against my wrist. With every step, my rapier would thump against my left leg. The air was cool and smelled of the sea. My boots were new enough to look good, yet old enough to be comfortable. My half-cloak was old and worn, yet it was Jhereg-grey and I could feel it dance behind me. The wind blew my hair back from my eyes. The streets were midafternoon quiet. The buildings were mostly shut, and—

There was a shadow that stood out unnaturally from the tall apartment complex on my left. I paused and saw that the shadown was beckoning me.

I approached it and said, "Hello, Kiera."

Morrolan looked disgusted; it was something he was good at. He said, "Sethra, you try."

She nodded; brisk, businesslike. "Morrolan has a cousin; her name is—"

"Aliera. Right; I got that."

"Aliera was caught in the explosion in Dragaera City that brought down the Imperium."

"Okay. I'm with you so far."

"I managed to save her."

"That's where you lose me. Didn't Morrolan say she was dead?"

"Well, yes."

"All right, then."

She drummed her fingers on the arm of her chair.

"You getting any more of this than I am, Loiosh?"

"Yeah, boss. I've already figured out that you're messed up with a couple of nut cases."

"Thanks loads."

At last Sethra said, "Death isn't as simple and straightforward as you may think it is. She is dead, but her soul has been preserved. It's been lost since the Interregnum, but we have located it, with your help, as well as the help of . . . well, some others. Yesterday, it was finally recovered."

"Okay, fine. Then why the trip to Deathgate Falls?" I had to suppress a shudder as I said the words.

"We need to have a living soul to work with, if not a living body. The body would be better, but the Necromancer can supply us with . . . well, never mind." Her voice trailed off, and consternation passed over her face.

"There you go again," I said. "First you say you have her soul, then you say—"

"The soul," said Sethra Lavode, "isn't as simple and

straightforward as you may think it is."

"Great," I said. I'm not sure, but I think Chaz might have smiled a bit. "Well, okay, how did it end up in the staff?"

"It's complicated. Loraan put it there, though. He found it right after the Interregnum, in a peasant's field somewhere. Now—"

"How did you know what the staff looks like?"

She gave me a scornful glance. "I can manage elementary divination, thank you."

"Oh. Well, excuse me for living, all right?"

"I might."

"So what is the state of her soul at the moment?"

She was silent for a few moments. Then she said, "Have you ever had cause to use a Morganti weapon?"

I held my face expressionless. "Maybe."

"In any case, you are familiar with them?"

"Yeah."

"Are you aware that Morganti weapons cannot destroy the soul of someone who is already dead?"

"Hmmm. I guess I've never thought about it. I've never had cause to go sticking Morganti weapons into corpses. It makes sense, though, I suppose."

"It's true. And yet the soul is still there, or else revivification would not be possible."

"Okay. I'll buy that."

"And are you aware that sometimes the bodies of those highly respected by their House are sent over Deathgate Falls, there to walk the Paths of the Dead?"

"I've heard that, too."

"So you can understand—"

"I understand that Easterners aren't allowed to enter the Paths of the Dead, and that, in any case, no one except the Empress Zerika has emerged alive."

"Both true," said Sethra. "But those two facts, taken together, may indicate that an *Easterner* would be allowed to—"

"May?"

She hesitated. "I think likely."

"Great. And, for doing this, I get exactly what?"

"We can pay—"

"I don't want to hear. Certain amounts of money are so high they become meaningless. Any less than that and I won't do it."

The two of them exchanged looks.

Morrolan said, "We'd very much like to convince you. It means a great deal to us, and there is no one else who can do it."

"This conversation sounds really familiar." I said. "You two had this in mind from the beginning, didn't you?"

"We considered it a possibility," said the Dark Lady of Dzur Mountain.

"And now you're saying that you'll kill me if I don't do it."

"No," said Morrolan. "Only that we'll be very grateful if you do."

They were learning how to deal with me. This could be good or bad, I suppose. I said, "Your gratitude would be nice, but if I'm already dead—"

"I think you can survive," said Sethra.

"How?"

"I've been there. I can tell you which paths to take and which to avoid, and warn you of dangers you are likely to encounter and how to protect yourself. That will leave you with only one danger, and I think the fact that you are an Easterner, who doesn't belong there, will be enough to—"

"What danger is that?"

"From those who run the place. The Lords of Judgment."

I didn't like the sound of that. There was a sharp intake of breath from Chaz, who'd been standing in his usual position during the whole interchange. I said, "The Lords of Judgment?"

"You know," said Sethra. "The gods."

I noticed that the stiletto I'd stuck in the ground was vibrating, and I wondered what that meant. After a moment, I detected a low-pitched hum. I concentrated on it until I could pick out the beats.

Beats . . .

Now, there was an idea.

I concentrated on the rhythm and held out my left hand, palm up. I concentrated on the humming and held out my right hand, palm up. I brought my hands together, turning them over so the palms met. Behind me, I felt Loiosh spreading his wings and collapsing them. My eyes closed as if of their own accord. I realized I was starting to feel fatigued, which frightened me, and I still had a great deal to do.

I don't know which changed, but now the humming worked with the rhythm I'd established.

I wondered how I'd write this up in a spell book, if I ever chose to do so.

"Fine," I said. "No problem. You mean I have nothing at all to worry about except a few gods? Well, in that case I don't see how it could go wrong. Sure, sign me up."

I was being sarcastic, in case it escaped you. I found myself glancing over at Chaz to see if he appreciated it, but I couldn't tell.

Sethra said, "I don't think it's quite as gruesome as that."

"Oh."

Morrolan said, "Show him the staff."

"I can see it from here," I said, looking at it next to Sethra's hand. Sethra ignored my comment and picked it up, held it out to me.

I said, "This person's soul is in there?"

"Yes," said Sethra. "Take it."

"Why?"

"To see if you feel anything."

"What am I supposed to feel?"

"Perhaps nothing. You won't know unless you hold it."

I sighed and took the thing. Since she'd spoken about feeling something, I was very much aware of the smooth finish, and that the thing was slightly cold. I'd held it before, but I'd been rather busy at the time. It was a light-colored wood, probably diamond willow.

"Feel anything, Loiosh?"

"I'm not sure, boss. Maybe. I think so."

Then I became aware of it, too. Yes, there was some sort of presence, seemingly dwelling at my fingertips. Strange. I was even getting a vague sense of personality; fiery, quick-tempered. A Dragon, certainly.

Also, to my surprise, I felt an instant sympathy; I'm still not sure why. I handed the staff back to Sethra and said, "Yeah, I felt something."

She said, "Well?"

"Well, what?"

"Will you do it?"

"Are you crazy? You've said no one except Zerika has—"

"I've also explained why I think you'll live through it."

I snorted. "Sure. All right, I'll do it—if you'll go along to protect me."

"Don't be absurd," snapped Sethra. "If I could go, there would be no need for you in the first place."

"Fine," I said. "Then I'll take Morrolan." I smirked, which I'm beginning to think is always an error when dealing with Dragonlords. I think I caught Chaz smirking, but I can't be sure.

Sethra and Morrolan exchanged glances. Then, "Very well," said Morrolan. "I agree."

I said, "Wait a minute—"

Sethra said, "Morrolan, the Lords of Judgment won't let you leave."

"Then so be it."

Sethra said, "But—"

I said, "But—"

"We'll leave tomorrow," Morrolan told me. "We'd best get you back at once to prepare for the journey."

Kiera the Thief's longish face was mostly concealed by a cowl as she towered over me, and her voice was low, not quite a whisper. "Hello, Vlad."

"Thank you."

She said, "So you know."

"I know it must have been you who spoke to Nielar about me. Thanks."

"I hope I'm doing you a favor," she said.

"Me, too. Why do you think you might not be?"

"Working for the Jhereg can be dangerous."

"I beat up Dragaerans anyway, every chance I get. Why not get paid for it?"

She studied my face. "Do you hate us so much?"

"Them, not you."

"I am Dragaeran."

"You still aren't one of them."

"Perhaps not."

"In any case, I need to make money if I'm going to stay out of the Easterners' ghetto."

"I know." I saw the flash of her teeth. "It wouldn't be proper for you to live there. You are a nobleman, after all."

I smiled back.

She said, "There are things I can teach you that will help."

"I'd like that," I said. "You're very kind."

"I like you."

She'd said that before. I often wondered why. I wondered

how old she was, too. But these were questions I didn't ask.

I said, "Well, wish me luck."

"Yes. There are a few things I should tell you now, though."

I was anxious to get going, but I'm not stupid. Kiera the Thief doesn't waste words. I said, "All right."

"The important thing is this, Vlad: Don't let your anger get the best of you. Dead men can't pay, and you won't earn if you don't deliver. And if you can get what you want without hurting someone, your employer will appreciate it. You may not realize it, but every time a Jhereg has to use violence, he's taking chances. They don't like that. Okay?"

"Okay." As she spoke, it struck me that in less than an hour, probably, I was going to be facing down and perhaps attacking someone I'd never met before. It seemed awfully cold-blooded. But, well, tough. I said, "What else?"

"Do you know anything about the Left Hand of the Jhereg?"

"Ummm . . . the what?"

"You don't, then. Okay. The Organization as you know it makes its money by providing goods and services that are either illegal or highly taxed, right?"

"I guess so. I'd never thought of it that way, but sure."

"Think of it that way. Now, the one exception is sorcery. There are sorcerous activities that are, as you know, illegal. Sorcerously aiding another illegal act, bending someone's will, and so forth." She spread her palms. "As the Demon says, 'Whenever they make a new law, they create a new business.' "

"Who said that?"

"The Demon."

"Who's he?"

"Never mind. In any case, the Left Hand of the Jhereg is mostly made up of women—I'm not sure why. They deal in illegal magic."

"I see."

"Stay away from them. You aren't up to fighting them, and you don't know enough to protect yourself from their machinations."

I said, "Yeah. I'll remember. Thanks, Kiera."

Her cowl nodded. She peered at me from within, then said, "Good luck, Vlad." She merged with the shadow of the building and was gone.

How ought one to prepare for a journey to the land of the dead?

I mean, I know how to get ready to go out on the town, and I know how to get ready to kill someone, and I even have some idea of how to prepare for a night spent in the jungle. But if you're going to visit the shades of the once living, the servitors of the dead, and the gods, what do you want to bring with you? How ought you to dress?

I wore my Jhereg colors, with a stylized jhereg on the back of the grey cloak I wear when I want to carry concealed this and that with me, and black Eastern riding boots that are comfortable, even if I wasn't going to be doing any riding—which was just as well. I've been on horseback before and if I never am again, that'll be fine. Just don't tell my grandfather I said that. He thinks Fenarians are supposed to be naturally great horsemen.

I wondered at Morrolan's agreement to accompany me. From everything I understood, his chances of emerging alive were worse than mine, and mine didn't seem to be all that good. I mean, Sethra had never actually *said* I'd be safe from the gods.

The gods. This was silly. I had occasionally joined my grandfather in our private family rituals, asking for the protection of Verra, the Demon Goddess, but I'd never been more than half convinced of her existence. Many Easterners I knew believed in one or more of the gods, and even those who didn't dropped their voices when naming them. But *all* Dragaerans seemed to believe in them, and spoke about them in such matter-of-fact tones that I wondered if, to a Dragaeran, the term "god" was all but meaningless. Someday, I decided, I'd have to investigate this.

Or perhaps I was going to find out during this journey. Which thought reminded me that I ought to be preparing. Morrolan had said the journey there should only take a few

days, as we would teleport to a point fairly close to Deathgate
Falls. Water would be available as we walked, as would
food. The weather was unpredictable, but my cloak was
fairly warm when pulled around me, fairly cool when thrown
back, and waterproof.

"*Any thoughts about what I should bring along?*"

"*An enchanted dagger, boss. Just in case.*"

"*I always carry one. What else?*"

"*That chain thing.*"

"*Hmmm. Yeah. Good idea.*"

"*Witch supplies?*"

"*I don't know. That's what I'm asking you.*"

"*No, I mean, are you going to bring supplies for spells?*"

"*Oh. I guess so.*"

So I got these things together, threw in some eddiberries
in case I needed to sleep, some kelsch leaves in case I
needed to stay awake, then reached out for contact with
Morrolan. It took quite a while since I didn't know him
terribly well, but at last we were in touch.

"*I'll be ready in an hour,*" I told him.

"*That will be fine,*" he said. "*Where should we meet?*"

I thought about this, then told him, "*There's this tavern
called Ferenk's in South Adrilankha.*"

Every time I visit a shoemaker I'm given to wonder how
anyone's shoes can come out well. That is, I've never seen
a shoemaker's place that wasn't as dark as Verra's Hell,
nor a shoemaker who didn't squint as if he were half blind.

The remains of the clothing on this particular shoemaker
claimed him for the House of the Chreotha, as did his longish
face and stubby fingers. The amount of grime under his
nails would have been sufficient for a garden. The hair on
his head was thin and grey; his eyebrows were thick and
dark. The room smelled heavily of leather and various oils
and I can't say what it looked like save that it was dark and
gloomy.

The Chreotha gave me a silent grunt (I can't describe it
any better that that) and indicated a spot of gloom that turned
out to contain a chair made of pieces of leather stretched

across a wooden frame. I sat down in it carefully, but it didn't seem about to collapse, so I relaxed. It was a bit small for a Dragaeran, which was pleasant since Dragaerans are taller than humans and it's annoying to sit in a chair designed for someone larger.

The shoemaker shuffled out of the room, presumably to let Nielar know I was there. Nielar was the guy who had hired me, after an unpleasant introduction involving a game of shereba that ran in the back of his building. Kiera had, I had gathered, intervened on my behalf, so I was showing up to work for him. I was also supposed to be meeting a partner.

"You must be Vlad Taltos," he said.

I jumped and almost drew the dagger from my sleeve.

"Mama?"

"It's all right, Loiosh."

He was sitting right across from me, and I'd somehow missed him in the dim light. He had a bit of a smirk on his face, probably from seeing me jump, but I resolved not to hate him right away. "Yes," I said. "I believe your name is Kragar?"

"I believe so, also. Since we both believe it, we might as well assume it's true."

"Ummm . . . right."

He watched me, still with the same sardonic expression. I wondered if he was trying to make me mad enough to attack him, to see if I could control myself. If so, I resented being tested. If not, he was just a jerk.

He said, "There's a guy who owes Nielar some money. Not all that much; forty imperials. But he's being stubborn. If we can get it, we split four imperials." I kept my face blank, while being amazed that my co-worker didn't think forty imperials was much money. This, I decided, might bode well for my future.

He continued, "Shall we go?" As he said this, he handed me what turned out to be a smooth, round stick, maybe an inch and a half in diameter and two feet long. I wrapped my hand around it. It was heavy enough to hurt someone. He continued, "Nielar said you already know how to use this."

"I guess so," I said, hefting the thing. "It is rather like a chair leg."

"What?"

"Never mind." I smirked back at him, feeling a bit cocky all of a sudden. "Let's go."

"Right."

As we headed out the door I said, "You'll do the talking, right?"

"No," he said. "You will."

"How long will you be gone, Vlad?"

"I don't know, Kragar. You're just going to have to take care of things as best you can. If I'm lucky, I'll be back in three or four days. If I'm not, I won't be back at all."

He chewed on his lip, a gesture I think he picked up from me. "I hope you're getting something for this."

"Yeah," I said. "Me, too."

"Well, good luck."

"Thanks."

Loiosh and I made our way to Ferenk's. The host recognized me at once and managed to keep a scowl off his face. When Morrolan came in, however, I could see that he drew his lips back and almost hissed. I smiled and said, "Two, please. We want dead bodies and seaweed. I'm sure you still know how to pour them."

He did, and I was pleased that Morrolan liked Fenarian peach brandy, but a little disappointed that he already knew about it, and even called it by its Fenarian name. However, he hadn't known that Ferenk's existed. I think he enjoyed being the only Dragaeran in the place, too. I remembered meeting Kiera there (by chance? Ha!) and wondered how the regulars would take to having Dragaerans drop by, and what sort of reputation I'd acquire at the place. At any rate, Morrolan enjoyed the experience more than Ferenk did.

Tough.

We walked out the door after a couple of glasses each. Then Morrolan stopped. I stood next to him. He closed his eyes and held himself still, then nodded to me. I braced myself, and South Adrilankha vanished. I expected to feel nauseous, and I was.

I hate that.

The target lived about half a mile away. To kill time as we walked, I asked Kragar to tell me about him.

"I don't know much, Vlad. He's an Orca, and he's owed Nielar the money for quite a while."

"An Orca? That's nice to hear."

"Why?"

"Nothing," I said. He glanced at me quickly but didn't comment. "Is he big?"

Kragar shrugged. "What's the difference? Hit him hard enough and he'll go down."

"Is that what we want to do?" I asked, remembering Kiera's advice. "Start swinging?" I discovered I was feeling nervous. When I'd taken to beating up the Dragaerans who'd been beating me up, it always happened suddenly. I'd never actually set out to get one. It makes a difference.

Kragar said, "Up to you."

I stopped. "What is this? You've done this before; I haven't. Why am I making all the decisions?"

"That was my deal when I agreed to work for Nielar—that I never have to give an order."

"Huh? Why?"

"None of your business."

I stared at him. Then I noticed that the House of the Dragon was so clearly marked on his face I couldn't understand how I'd missed it before. There was almost certainly a story there.

As we resumed our walk, I pondered Kragar. He was almost exactly seven feet tall, had medium straight brown hair, brown eyes, and, well, really nothing else to distinguish him. Questions buzzed around my head, without attending answers. Where had he come from? How had he found himself in the Jhereg?

He touched my shoulder and pointed to a building. It bore the insignia of a wolf howling and seemed to be a pretty nice place from the outside. The inside was also in good repair. We walked through the main room, earning some scowls from patrons who didn't like Easterners,

Jhereg, or both. We went up the stairs. As we climbed the three flights and turned to the left, I was still wondering about Kragar, and I continued to wonder until we had clapped outside the door and it had opened.

The Orca looked at me and blinked. He said, "Yeah, whiskers?"

Oh. Here I was. I'd been so distracted thinking about Kragar that I hadn't considered how to approach the Orca. Well, since I didn't know what to say, I hit him in the stomach with the stick. He said something like "Oooph" and buckled over. I think I might have cracked a couple of ribs; my aim wasn't all that good. I wondered if he was the right guy.

In any case, the top of his head was right below me. I almost brought the club down, but I remembered Kiera's words and didn't. Instead I put my foot against him and pushed. He fell over backward and it occurred to me how easy it had been to take the guy when he wasn't expecting an attack.

He rolled over onto his stomach, coughing. I'd gotten him pretty good, but Orca are tough. I put my foot on his back. Kragar came up next to me and put a foot on the guy's neck. I removed my foot and walked around, then knelt down in front of him. He seemed startled and craned his neck, looking around. I guess he hadn't realized there were two of us. Then he glared at me.

On impulse I reached into my cloak, pulled out my jhereg, and held him in front of the guy. I said, "Hungry, Loiosh?"

"Mama?"

"It's okay."

Loiosh flicked a tongue out toward the Orca, whose eyes were now wide with fear. I said to him, "You owe people money."

"Let me up," he croaked. "I'll give it to you."

"No. I don't want it. I want you to pay it. If you don't, we'll come back. You have twenty-four hours. Do you understand?"

He managed to nod.

"Good." I stood up and put Loiosh away. I headed out

to the stairs, Kragar behind me.

Once we'd left, Kragar said, "Why didn't you take the money?"

I said, "Huh? I don't know. I guess it would have felt like robbing him."

Kragar laughed. Well, I suppose on reflection it was funny. I was trembling a bit. If Kragar had commented on it I would have smashed his face in, but he didn't.

I had settled down by the time we were back where we'd started. The shoemaker wasn't around when we returned, but Nielar was. He studied me, ignoring Kragar, and said, "Well?"

I said, "I don't know."

"You don't know?"

"Does the guy have dark hair that he wears plastered straight back, kind of a wide face, big shoulders, a short neck, and a little white scar across his nose?"

"I've never noticed the scar, but, yeah, that sounds right."

"Then we talked to the right guy."

"That's good. What did you talk about?"

"We asked him if he wouldn't mind paying what he owes."

"What did he say?"

"He seemed to consider the matter carefully."

Nielar nodded slowly. "Okay. Where's Kragar?"

"Right here," said Kragar, sounding amused.

"Oh. What do you think?"

"He'll pay. We gave him a day." He paused, then, "Vlad does good work."

Nielar studied me for a moment. "Okay," he said. "I'll be in touch with you guys."

I nodded and walked out of the shop. I wanted to thank Kragar, but I couldn't find him. I shrugged and went home to feed Loiosh and wait.

I got home feeling a bit exhausted, but good. I was pretty pleased with life for a change. I fed Loiosh some cow's milk and fell asleep on the couch with him on my stomach. Perhaps I was smiling.

The first thing I noticed was the sky. It was still the ugly reddish, orangish thing that hangs over the Empire, but it was higher and somehow cleaner. We were surrounded by grasses that reached my waist. There was not a tree or a mountain or a building in sight.

We stood there for a few minutes, Morrolan politely remaining silent while I took several deep breaths, trying to recover from the aftereffects of the teleport. I looked around, and something occurred to me. I tried to figure it out, then said, "All right, I give up. How did you get a teleport fix on a spot with absolutely no distinguishing features?"

He smiled. "I didn't. I just fixed on approximately where I wanted to go, visualized the area, and hoped nothing would be there."

I stared at him. He smiled back at me. "Well," I said after a while. "I guess it worked."

"I guess so. Shall we begin walking?"

"What direction?"

"Oh. Right." He closed his eyes and turned his head slowly from side to side. He finally pointed off in a direction that looked like any other. "That way," he said.

Loiosh flew overhead. The breeze was cool but not chilly. Morrolan cut back on the length of his strides so he wouldn't keep getting ahead of me.

I tried not to think of the whithers or the wherefores of the journey, but the staff in Morrolan's left hand kept reminding me.

9 –

*The object of my desire was there, and I needed it here.
I had forged most of those links already: there was rep-
resented by a quivering knife, here was the glowing rune.
But more, I had to break a spatial barrier and cause a thing
to exist that did not, while destroying a thing that did, yet
in fact do neither of these, merely cause a spatial readjust-
ment.*

If that sounds confusing to listen to, try doing it.

*I had become a thing of rhythm and wave, sight and
sound, of a wavering landscape and a humming knife and
a glowing rune and a pulse.*

*They were united in my will and in the symbols before
me. Think of it as a cosmic juggling act in the mind, and
you'll have about the right idea.*

I was getting to the hard part.

We rested under the open sky that night, which sounds
romantic but wasn't, and ought to have been chilly but
Morrolan fixed that. I don't like the hard ground, but it was
better than it could have been. Morrolan doesn't snore, and
if I do he never mentioned it.

We didn't have any cooking gear with us, but we didn't need any, what with Morrolan being along. I drank tea from an invisible glass and ate bread that hadn't been with us the night before and berries that were growing all around us, nice and ripe.

I stared at the slowly diminishing cylinder of liquid in my hand and said, "Now, that's the sort of magic I'd like to be able to do."

Morrolan didn't deign to answer. The good stuff is always difficult. We resumed our walk. It was a nice warm day, and I saw the distant peaks of mountains.

I said, "Is that our destination?"

Morrolan nodded.

I said, "How long a walk would you say that is?"

"It doesn't matter. When we get close enough to make out a few details, we'll teleport again."

"Oh."

It was, I have to say, hard to stay hostile to the man next to me, if only because the day was nice and the walk so pleasant. Birds sang, the wind rustled, and all that sort of thing.

Loiosh flew above me and occasionally disappeared for brief intervals when he found something to scavenge. I could feel that he was enjoying himself. From time to time I would catch sight of wild jhereg, flying high above us, but Loiosh and I ignored them.

We stopped around midday, and Morrolan conjured more food for us. I don't know whether he was creating it from thin air or teleporting it from somewhere. I suspect the former because it tasted pretty bland. As we ate, Morrolan studied the mountains that were slowly growing before us as we walked. As we stood up, he announced, "Not yet. We need to be closer."

That was fine by me. We resumed our walk, and all was well with the world.

I wondered if I'd be dead by this time tomorrow.

I got a message the next day to see Nielar. This time I was to meet him at his office—in back of the shereba game, which was in turn in back of a small sorcery supply shop.

I was admitted at once, without having to identify myself ("When the Easterner shows up, let him in"), and Nielar nodded me to a chair.

He said, "Let's wait for Kragar."

Kragar said, "I'm here already."

We both did double takes, then Nielar cleared his throat. "Right," he said. "Well, here's four imperials for you two to split. And, Vlad, here's another four for your first week's pay. You work for me now, all right? I want you here tomorrow evening to keep an eye on the shereba game."

I took the eight coins and gave Kragar two of them. I had just earned, in one day, more than I would have taken in at the restaurant in several weeks. I said, "Right, boss."

Morrolan stopped suddenly, with no warning, and he stood still, staring off ahead and a little to his left. I looked in that direction and saw nothing except unbroken plain, with more mountains in the distance.

"Check it, Loiosh."

"Right, boss."

We stood there for most of a minute, Morrolan continuing to stare, Loiosh flying off in the indicated direction. Then Loiosh said, *"Boss, you've got to see this."*

"Very well. Show me." I closed my eyes and let Loiosh fill my brain.

Yeah, it was quite a sight.

There were these beings, maybe two dozen of them, and I've never seen anyone or anything run so fast. They had four legs and from the waist down appeared to be feline, smaller than the dzur, perhaps the size of the tiassa but without wings. From the waist up they appeared human. They carried spears.

"Cat-centaurs, Loiosh?"

"I guess so, boss. I hadn't known they were real."

"Nor had I. Interesting."

"I think they're heading toward us."

"Yeah."

I broke the connection, and by now I could see them with my own eyes, as a gradually resolving blur in the distance. Verra, but they were fast. I noted that Morrolan had not touched his sword, and I took some comfort from that. I began to hear them then; a very low rumble that made me realize I ought to have heard them some time ago. They were awfully quiet for their size.

They were suddenly stopped before us. The butt ends of their spears rested on the ground as they looked at us through human faces with expressions of mild curiosity. The spears had worked metal heads, which I decided was significant. I had the impression that they ran just because they wanted to. None of them were breathing hard. They stared at us, unblinking, like cats. They wore no clothing, but many of them carried pouches, tied around their backs and hanging down the sides. The muscles around their back legs were impressive as hell.

I said, "So, what else do you do for fun?"

Morrolan turned and glared at me. The cat-centaur who was at their head, and who was emphatically female, looked at me and smiled a little. "Chase things," she said. She spoke Dragaeran without any trace of accent.

Loiosh landed on my shoulder, and the leader's eyes widened. I said, "My name is Vlad Taltos."

Morrolan said, "I am Morrolan."

She said, "I am called Mist."

A cat-centaur with red eyes said, "That's because when she throws her spear—"

"Shut up, Brandy." There was some laughter, which included Loiosh, though only I was aware of that.

Mist said, "The jhereg on your shoulder—he is your friend?"

I said, "Yeah."

"Jhereg feed on dead cat-centaurs."

I said, "Dead men, too," which seemed to satisfy her.

She said, "What brings you to the Forever Plains?"

Morrolan said, "We journey to Deathgate Falls," and the entire collection of cat-centaurs took a step back from us. I stooped down and picked and ate a strawberry, waiting.

After a moment, Mist said, "I assume you have good reason."

Morrolan started to answer, but another cat-centaur said, "No, they're just out on a lark."

Mist said, "Keep still, Birch."

I said, "Say, are those *real* spears?"

Morrolan said, "Shut up, Vlad."

Loiosh seemed about to have hysterics. Some of the cat-centaurs appeared to be in the same situation. Me, too. Morrolan and Mist caught each other's eyes and shook their heads sadly.

Mist said, "If you wait here, we're following a very large wild kethna. When we bring it down, we'll share it with you."

"We shall get a fire going," said Morrolan. Then, "Um, you *do* cook your meat, do you not?"

Brandy said, "No, we prefer to let the raw, fresh blood of our kill drip down our—"

"Shut up, Brandy," said Mist. "Yes, a fire would be nice."

"See you soon, then," said Morrolan.

"Quite soon, I expect," said Mist, and they turned and sped off the way they'd come.

There was a good tailor who lived near my flat. I went to see him late in the afternoon of the next day and ordered a full, grey cloak. I also ordered a new jerkin, with ribbing parallel to the collarbone. I lusted after a hat with a tall plume, but didn't get it.

The tailor said, "Come into some funds, eh?"

I didn't know what to say so I just gave him a terse nod. I don't know what he read into that, but his eyes widened just a bit, showing what could have been fear. A small thrill passed through me as I turned away and said, "I'll expect them in a week."

He said, "Yes, they'll be done." He sounded just a bit breathless.

I went a bit farther down the street and bought a brace of throwing knives. I resolved to start practicing with them.

Then I reported in to Nielar. He nodded to me and sent me to the room with the shereba game. Two days before, I'd been playing there, and a large Jhereg had thrown me out after I'd gotten into a tussle with another customer. Now I was sitting where the Jhereg had sat. I tried to look as relaxed and unconcerned as he'd been. I guess I was partially successful.

But, hell, I enjoyed it.

We lost most of the day eating and socializing with the cat-centaurs and enjoying it, although it got us no closer to our goal. I don't usually gamble, but these poor, uncivilized creatures didn't even know how to play S'yang Stones, so I had to show them, didn't I? We had a good medium of exchange, too, as there are certain cuts of kethna that are better than others. The cat-centaurs were fairly dexterous, so I quit when they were starting to catch on.

Mist said, "I suspect that I won't be thanking you for teaching us this game, in another few weeks."

"It's just harmless fun," I said between bites of my fresh-roasted winnings. As they say, gambling isn't fun; winning is fun.

It was fun exchanging banter with them, and I learned to know when I was pushing one too far by watching the tail, which would have been very strange if I'd stopped to think about it. Morrolan did some healing spells on three of the cat-centaurs whose left legs had been injured in one way or another. "There's been a rash of that lately," said Mist after thanking him.

"A curse?" said Morrolan.

"Just bad luck, I think."

"There's a lot of that going around," said Morrolan.

"Especially where you're going."

Morrolan shrugged. "I don't imagine you know much more about the place than we do."

"I usually avoid it."

"We would, too, if we could," said Morrolan.

Mist stared at the ground, her tail flicking. "Why are you going there?"

Morrolan said, "It's a long story."

Mist said, "We have time for long tales. Shut up, Brandy."

Morrolan seemed disinclined to talk about it, so a silence fell. Then a male I didn't recognize approached Mist and handed her something. She took and studied it. I hadn't noticed before how long and sleek her hands were, and her fingernails made me wince, recalling a girl I once knew. What Mist held seemed to be a piece of bone. After some study she said, "Yes. This will do." She handed it to Morrolan.

He took it, puzzled, while I went around behind him and stared at it over his shoulder. It probably had been broken from the skull of the kethna. It was very roughly square, about two inches on a side, and I could see some thin tracings on it. I could make nothing whatsoever of the markings.

Morrolan said, "Thank you. What—"

"Should you come across Kelchor in the Paths of the Dead, and show her this token, it may be that she'll protect you." She paused. "On the other hand, she may not."

"Gods are like that," said Morrolan.

"Aren't they, though," said Mist.

I had my doubts about whether either of them actually knew anything.

Here's something you can do, if you ever get the mood. Find a Dragaeran who isn't inclined to beat you up, and start talking about magic. Watch the curl of his lip when he hears about witchcraft. Then start discussing numbers associated with the art. Talk about how, with some spells, you want two black candles and one white one, other times you want two white ones and no black. Mention that, for instance, in one of the simpler love spells you must use three pinches of rosemary. The size of a "pinch" doesn't matter, but the number three is vital. In another spell you can tell him, you must speak in lines of nine syllables, although what you say doesn't matter.

Long about this time, he'll be unable to hide his contempt and he'll start going on about how silly it is to attach significance to numbers.

That's when you get to have your fun. Cock your head to the side, stare at him quizzically, and say, "Why is the Dragaeran population broken up into seventeen Great Houses? Why are there seventeen months in the Dragaeran year? Why is seventeen times seventeen years the minimum time for a House to hold the throne and the Orb, while the maximum is three thousand something, or seventeen times seventeen times seventeen? Why are there said to be seventeen Great Weapons?"

He will open his mouth and close it once or twice, shake his head, and say, "But seventeen is the mystical number."

Now you can nod wisely, your eyes twinkling, say, "Oh, I see," and walk away.

I mention this only because I have a little nagging feeling that the Dragaerans may be right. At least, it does seem that the number seventeen keeps popping up when I least expect it.

At any rate, I was seventeen years old the first time I was paid to kill a man.

We made our farewells to the cat-centaurs the next morning. Mist and Morrolan exchanged words that struck me as a bit formal and pompous on both sides. Brandy and I enjoyed making fun of them, though, and Loiosh had a few remarks as well.

Then Mist came up to me, her tail swishing, and she seemed to be smiling. She said, "You are a good companion."

I said, "Thanks."

She paused, and I was afraid she was gathering herself together for some speech that I'd have trouble keeping a straight face for, but then she lowered her spear until its point was a few inches from my breast. Loiosh tensed to spring. Mist said, "You may touch my spear."

Oh. Peachy. I had to restrain myself from glancing over at Brandy to see if he was sniggering. But what the hell. I touched it, then drew my rapier. I said, "You may touch my sword."

She did so, solemnly. And you know, all sarcasm aside, I was moved by the whole thing. Mist gave Morrolan and me a last nod, then she led her friends or tribe or companions, or whatever, back into the plain. Morrolan and I watched them until they were out of sight, then got our things together and set off for the mountains.

After walking a few more hours, Morrolan stopped again

and stared straight ahead, toward the base of the mountains.
He said, "I think I can make out enough details to teleport
us safely."

I said, "Better be sure. Let's walk another few hours."

He glanced at me. "I'm sure."

I kept my moan silent and merely said, "Fine. I'm ready."

He stared hard at the mountains ahead of us as I drew
next to him. All was still except for our breathing. He raised
his hands very slowly, exhaled loudly, and brought his arms
down. There was the sickening lurch in my stomach and I
closed my eyes. I felt the ground change beneath my feet,
opened my eyes again, looked around, and almost fell.

We were on a steep slope and I was facing down. Loiosh
shrieked and dived into my cloak as I fought to recover my
balance. After flailing around for a while I did so.

The air was cool here, and very biting. Behind us was
an incredible expanse of green. All around us were mountains, hard and rocky. I managed to sit without losing my
balance. Then, using my backpack as a pillow, I lay on my
back on the slope, waiting for the nausea to pass.

After a few minutes, Morrolan said, "We're about as
close as we can get."

I said, "What does that mean?"

"As you approach Greymist Valley, sorcery becomes
more difficult. From the time you reach the Deathgate, it
is impossible."

I said, "Why is that?"

"I don't know."

"Are you certain it's true, or is it just rumor?"

"I'm certain. I was at the top of the falls with Zerika,
holding off some local brigands while she made her descent.
If I could have used sorcery, I would have."

I said, "Brigands?"

"Yes."

"Charming."

"I don't see any at the moment."

"Great. Well, if they return, they may recognize you and
leave us alone."

"None of those will return."

"I see."

"There are far fewer now than during the Interregnum, Vlad. I wouldn't worry. Those were wilder times."

I said, "Do you miss them?"

He shrugged. "Sometimes."

I continued looking around and noticed a few jhereg circling in the distance. I said, *"Loiosh, did you see the jhereg?"*

He said, *"I saw them."* He was still hiding inside my cloak.

"What's the matter, chum?"

"Boss, did you see them?"

I looked up at them again but couldn't figure out the problem until one of them landed on a cliff far above us. Then, suddenly, the scale made sense.

"By the Phoenix, Loiosh! Those things are bigger than I am."

"I know."

"I don't believe it. Look at them!"

"No."

I stood up slowly, put my pack on, and nodded to Morrolan. We continued up the slope for another couple of hours, then it leveled off. The view was magnificent, but Loiosh couldn't appreciate it. From time to time, the giant jhereg would come close enough to us to give me the creeps, so I couldn't blame him. After another hour or so, we came to a wide, fast stream coming from up a slope we didn't take.

Morrolan turned with the stream, and in a couple more hours it had become a small river. By dark it was a big river, and we found a place to make our last camp.

As we were settling in for the night, I said, "Morrolan, does this river have a name?"

He said, "Blood River."

I said, "Thought so," and drifted off to sleep.

After walking for an hour or so the next morning, we had followed it to Deathgate Falls.

10 =

I suppose I would have composed a chant if I'd had time, but I'm not very good at that. No chance for it now, though. Loiosh lent me strength, which I poured into the enchantment, creating more tension. The rhythm became stronger, and the candle suddenly flared before me.

Scary.

I concentrated on it, turning the flare into a shower of sparks, which exploded into a globe of flickering nothing. I brought it together again, surrounding the candle flame with a rainbow nimbus. I didn't have to ask Loiosh to pick up and control it; I wanted him to and he did.

My breathing stilled; I felt my eyes narrow. I was relaxed, easy and part of things, no longer on the edge. This was a stage and it would pass, but I could use it while it lasted. Now was the time to forge the connection between source and destination, to establish the path along which reality would bend.

The knife quivered, saying, "Start here." All right, fine. Start there and do what? I looked from knife to rune and back. I reached forward with my right hand, forefinger

*extended, and traced a line. I repeated the process. And
again.*

*I kept it up, always going from knife to rune. After a
while there was a line of flame connecting them.*

*It felt right. I raised my eyes. The landscape still wavered,
as if I were surrounded by unreality, ready to close in on
me. That could be pretty frightening, if I let it.*

Deathgate Falls has an exact geographical location; there-
fore, so do the Paths of the Dead, only they don't. Don't
ask me to explain that because I can't. I know that somewhere in the Ash Mountains is a very high cleft called
Greymist Valley. There is a possibly legendary assassin
named Mario Greymist who was named after the place, for
the number of people he sent there.

To this valley are brought the corpses of any Dragaeran
deemed important (and rich) enough for someone to make
the arrangements. The Blood River flows into the valley,
and over a waterfall, and that is the end of the matter as far
as the living are concerned.

The height of the waterfall has been reported by those
undead who have returned from the Paths. The reports say
it is a mere fifty feet, that it is a thousand feet, and any
number of distances in between. Your guess is as good as
mine, and I mean that.

No one has ever come to the foot of the falls by any route
except the cliff, though many, especially Hawks and Athyra,
have tried. For all intents and purposes, the foot of the falls
isn't in the same world as the lip. Volumes have been written
in the debate over whether this was set up by the gods, or
whether it is a naturally occurring phenomenon. To show
how futile it is, several of the gods have participated in the
debate on various sides.

Those few who leave the Paths of the Dead (undead such
as Sethra, and the Empress Zerika who got a special dispen-
sation) do not leave by means of the falls. Instead they
report finding themselves walking out through a long cave
they can never find later, or waking up at the foot of the
Ash Mountains, or lost in the Forbidden Forest, or even

walking along the seacoast a thousand miles away.

It isn't supposed to make sense, I suppose.

I stood next to the lip of the waterfall and looked out at an orangish horizon interrupted by the occasional jutting of rocky peaks. Below me grey fogs swirled and rose, obscuring the bottom hundreds of feet below. The din of the falls made talking all but impossible. The Blood River somehow turned white on its thundering way down.

I stepped back from the brink. Morrolan, next to me, did the same at almost the same instant. We walked away from it. The sound dropped off rapidly, and, just as quickly, the river widened and slowed, until only fifty feet from the falls it seemed like you could wade in it, and we could hear ourselves breathe.

This did not seem normal, but I saw no reason to ask about it.

Morrolan was glancing around him, an odd look on his face. I would have said wistful if I could have believed it of him. I noticed him staring at a pedestal set back about twenty feet from the water. I came up next to him, expecting, I guess, to see the name of some dead guy, and to ask Morrolan if it was a relative. Instead, I saw a stylized dzur head.

I looked a question at Morrolan. He pointed back toward the river, where I noticed a flat spot. "It is here where the remains of those of the House of the Dzur are sent onto the river to go over the falls."

"Splash," I said. "But at least they're dead already. I doubt it bothers them."

He nodded and continued to stare at the pedestal. I said, trying to sound casual, "Know any Dzurlords who've come this way?"

"Sethra," he said.

I blinked. "I thought she was a Dragon."

Morrolan shrugged and turned away, and we continued walking away from the falls. We came upon another flat spot against the river, which was starting to curve now, and I saw a stylized chreotha, then later a hawk, then a dragon. Morrolan paused there for some moments, and I backed up and gave him room for whatever he was feeling. His hand was white where he gripped the staff that contained some form of the soul of his cousin, in some condition or another.

Loiosh still hid inside my cloak, and I realized that the giant jhereg still circled above us, and we could hear their cries from time to time. Presently, Morrolan joined me in staring at the dark swirling waters. Birds made bird sounds, and the air was clear and very sharp. It was a somber, peaceful place, and it seemed to me that this was a calculated effect, achieved I'm not sure how. Yet, certainly, it worked.

Morrolan said, "Dragons usually use boats."

I nodded and tried to picture a small fishing boat, then a skip like they use along the Sunset River above the docks, and finally a rowboat, which made the most sense. I could see it floating down the stream until it reached the waterfall, and over, lost.

I said, "Then what happens?"

Morrolan said, "Eventually the body comes to rest along the shore, below the falls. After a few days, the soul awakens and takes whatever it finds on the body that it can use, and begins the journey to the Halls of Judgment. The journey can take hours or weeks. Sometimes it lasts forever. It depends on how well the person has memorized the Paths for his House while he is alive, and on what he meets on the way, and how he handles it." He paused. "We may meet some of those who have been wandering the Paths forever. I hope not. I imagine it would be depressing."

I said, "What about us?"

"We will climb down next to the falls."

"Climb?"

"I have rope."

"Oh," I said. "Well, that's all right, then."

I had been in the Organization nearly a year and it was getting to where I was feeling quietly good at what I did. I could threaten people without saying a word, just with a raised eyebrow or a smile, and they'd feel it. Kragar and I functioned well together, too. If the target started getting violent I'd just stand there while Kragar hit him, usually from behind. Then I'd inflict some minor damage on him and give him a lecture on pacifism.

It was working well, and life was going smoothly, until we heard about a guy named Tiev being found in an alley behind a tavern. Now, it is sometimes possible, although expensive, to return a corpse to life. But in this case Tiev had been cut in the back of the neck, severing his spine, which is something sorcerers can't deal with. He was carrying about twenty imperials when he was killed, and the money was still on his body.

Tiev, I heard, was working for a guy named Rolaan, and rumors had it that Tiev had been known to do assassinations. Rolaan was a powerful kind of guy, and Kragar mentioned hearing a rumor that another powerful kind of guy, named Welok the Blade, had ordered Tiev's killing. This was important to me because my boss worked for Welok—or, at least, he supposedly paid Welok a percentage of everything he earned.

A week later a guy named Lefforo was killed in a manner similar to Tiev. Lefforo worked directly for Welok and was, furthermore, someone I'd actually met, so that was hitting pretty close to home. People I'd see at my boss's place started looking nervous, and my boss implied to me that it would be a good idea not to wander around alone. I couldn't imagine what anyone had to gain from killing me, but I started staying home a lot. That was okay. I wasn't making so much money that I was anxious to go and spend it, and Loiosh was by now almost full grown, so it was fun to spend time training him. That is, I'd say, *"Loiosh, find the red ball in the bedroom,"* and he'd go off and come back with it in his claws. He'd stopped calling me *"Mama"* by then, but had picked up the habit of calling me "boss," I guess from the way I addressed my superior.

Anyway, a couple of weeks later, my boss asked to see me. I went over to his office, and he said, "Shut the door." I did. We were alone, and I started getting nervous.

He said, "Sit down, Vlad."

I sat down and said, "Yeah, boss?"

He licked his lips. "Any interest in doing some work for

me?" There was just a bit of emphasis on the word "work."

My mouth went dry. After close to a year, I'd picked up enough of the slang to know what he meant. I was surprised, startled, and all that. It had never occurred to me that anyone would ask me to do that. On the other hand, saying no never crossed my mind. I said, "Sure."

He seemed to relax a little. "Okay. Here's the target." He handed me a drawing of a Dragaeran. "Know him?"

I shook my head.

He said, "Okay. His name is Kynn. He's an enforcer for, well, it doesn't matter. He's tough, so don't take any chances. He lives on Potter's Market Street, near Undauntra. He hangs out in a place called Gruff's. Know it?"

"Yeah."

"He bounces for a brothel three doors up from there most Endweeks, and he does collecting and bodyguard work pretty often, but he doesn't keep to a schedule. Is that enough?"

I said, "I guess so."

"He isn't traveling alone much these days, so you may have to wait for a chance. That's okay. Take as much time as you need to get it right, and don't let yourself be seen. Be careful. And I don't want him revivifiable, either. Can you handle that?"

"Yeah."

"Good."

"Is he going to have alarms in his flat?"

"Huh? Oh. Stay away from his flat."

"Why?"

"You don't do that."

"Why not?"

He looked at me for a moment, then said, "Look, he's a Jhereg, right?"

"Right."

"And you're a Jhereg, right?"

"Right."

"You don't do that."

"Okay."

"You also don't go near him while he's in or around a temple, an altar, or anywhere like that."

"All right."

"He's married, too. You don't touch him while his wife's around."

"All right. Do I get to use both hands?"

"Don't be funny."

"I don't get to do that, either, huh?"

Loiosh, who'd taken to wandering around on my shoulder, stared at the drawing and hissed. I guessed he was picking up on more than I thought. My boss started at this, but didn't comment. He handed me a purse. I took it and it seemed very heavy.

I said, "What's this?"

"Your payment. Twenty-five hundred imperials."

When I could speak again, I said, "Oh."

We built a fire considerably back from the river and cooked the last of the meat from the kethna. We ate it slowly, in silence, each busy with his own thoughts. Loiosh sneaked out of my cloak long enough to grab a morsel and dived back in.

We rested and cleaned up after eating, then Morrolan suggested we rest some more.

"Some have said it is bad luck to sleep while in the Paths. Others have said it is impossible. Still others have said nothing on the subject." He shrugged. "I see no reason to take chances; I should like to be as well rested as possible before we begin."

Later I watched Morrolan as he fashioned a harness to hold the staff to his back, so he could have both hands free for climbing. I unwrapped my chain from around my left wrist and looked at it. I swung it around a few times. It was behaving just like any other chain, which was either because of where we were or because it hadn't anything else to do. I put it away again, considered testing what Morrolan had said by attempting sorcery, changed my mind.

I caught Morrolan staring at me. He said, "Have you named it?"

"The chain? No. What's a good name?"

"What does it do?"

"When I used it before, it worked like a shield against whatever that wizard was throwing at me. How about Spellbreaker?"

Morrolan shrugged and didn't answer.

"I like it, boss."

"Okay. I'll stick with it. I have trouble being all that serious about giving a name to a piece of chain."

Morrolan said, "Let's be about it, then."

I nodded, put Spellbreaker back around my wrist, and stood up. We walked back to the falls, our voices once again drowned by proximity to the falls. I noticed there was a pedestal quite close to the edge, and saw an athyra carved on it. Morrolan tied one end of his rope around this pedestal which some might think in poor taste, I don't know.

The rope seemed thin and was very long. He threw the other end down the cliff. My mouth was dry. I said, "Is the rope going to be strong enough?"

"Yes."

"Okay."

"I'll go first," said Morrolan.

"Yeah. You go down and hold 'em off while I set up the ballista."

He turned his back to the falls, wrapped his hands around the rope, and began to lower himself. I had this momentary urge to cut the rope and run, but instead I gripped the rope tightly and got ready to go over. I turned and yelled down over the roar of the falls, "Any last-minute advice on this, Morrolan?"

His voice was barely audible, but I think he said, "Be careful, it's wet here."

I left my payment for the work in my flat and wandered toward Gruff's. On the way over, I wondered what I'd do there. My first thought had been to find him there, wait for him to leave, and kill him. In retrospect, this wouldn't have been that bad a plan, as the sight of death tends to make witnesses confused about those who cause it. But I was worried that, as an Easterner, I was likely to stand out in the crowd, which meant he'd notice me, which I knew wasn't good. By the time I got there, I still hadn't figured out what to do, so I stood in the shadow of a building across the street from it, thinking.

I hadn't come up with anything two hours or so later, when I saw him leave in the company of another Dragaeran in Jhereg colors. Just because it seemed like the thing to do, I concentrated on my link to the Imperial Orb and noted the time. I waited for them to get a block ahead of me, then set out after them. I followed them to a building which I assumed was the home of my target's friend.

My target.

The words had peculiar echo in my head.

I shook off the thought and noted that Kynn and his friend seemed to be saying good-bye. Then the friend went upstairs, leaving Kynn alone on the street. This could be good luck for me, because now Kynn had to walk back to his own place alone, which gave me several blocks to come up behind him and kill him.

I fingered the dagger next to my rapier. Kynn seemed to waver for a moment, then he became transparent and vanished.

He teleported, of course. Now that was just plain rude.

Teleports can be traced, but I'm not a good enough sorcerer to do so. Hire someone to do it? Who? The Left Hand of the Jhereg had sorcerers good enough, but they charged high, and Kiera's warning about them still echoed in my ears. And it would involve standing out there waiting for him on another occasion, as no sorcerer can work from a trail that cold.

I settled on cursing as the appropriate action, and did so silently for a moment. I'd wanted to get it done today, which on reflection was stupid, but I had the feeling that the money wasn't really mine until I'd done the work, and I could use that money. I could move to a nicer flat, I could pay for fencing lessons from an Eastern master, and sorcery lessons from a Dragaeran, which never came cheap, and —

No, not now. Now I had to think about how to earn it, not how to spend it. I returned to my flat and considered the matter.

• • •

The next time I climb down from somewhere on a rope, I think I'm going to try to arrange for it to be somewhere dry. I also want to be able to see the bottom.

Come to think of it, I'd rather not do it at all.

I don't care to guess how long the way down was. I suspect it was different for Morrolan than for me, and I don't want to know that. I'll admit I'm curious about what would have happened if we'd marked the rope, but we didn't.

The climb down was no fun at all. I tended to slip on the wet rope, and I was afraid I'd land on Morrolan, sending us both crashing down. First my hands stung from gripping the thing, then they ached, then I couldn't feel them, which scared me. Then I noticed that my arms were getting sore. We won't even mention the bruises and contusions my legs and body were sustaining from hitting the rocks on the side. I managed not to bang my head too hard or too often, which I think was quite an accomplishment.

Crap. Let's just say I survived.

The thing is, it was impossible to really determine where the bottom was, because not only was the first place my feet landed slippery, it seemed to be the point of a massive slab of rock tilted sideways, so I kept going.

It was a bit easier after that, though, and eventually I found myself in water, and Morrolan was next to me. The water was very cold. My teeth started chattering, and I saw that Morrolan's were, too, but I was too cold to be pleased about it. Loiosh angrily climbed onto my shoulder. The noise was still deafening, every inch of me was soaked, and my hands hurt like blazes from gripping the rope.

I put my mouth next to Morrolan's ear and yelled, "What now?"

He gestured a direction with his head and we struck out for it. After having developed a symbiotic relationship with that rope, it was hard to let go of it, but I did and started splashing after him. Loiosh took wing and flew just over my head. The mist kicked up by the waterfall made it impossible to see more than a couple of feet ahead of me. The current was strong, though, and tended somehow to keep Morrolan and me together, so I never lost sight of him.

I was too busy fighting the current and keeping track of Morrolan to be as scared as I ought to have been, but it wasn't actually all that long before my feet felt the bottom of the river, and then we were crawling up onto the bank, and then we collapsed, side by side.

11 —

My left hand froze, and some part of me was aware that it hovered over the rune. My right hand continued to drift without direction; then it, too, stopped. It was directly over the vibrating knife.

Time for one deep breath, which I let out slowly.

I don't think I'll ever again see so many corpses in one place. I don't especially want to, either, And they were all in different and interesting stages of decomposition. I'll forego the details, if you don't mind. I'd seen bodies before, and sheer number and variety makes them no more pleasant to look at.

I should mention one odd thing, though: there was no odor of decay. In fact, as I thought about it, I realized that the only smell I could detect was faint and sulfurous and seemed to come from the river, which was now fast and white-capped. The river also provided the only sounds I could hear as it sloshed its way over greyish rocks and up onto sandy banks, doing carvings in slate.

I felt Loiosh shivering inside of my cloak.

"You okay?"

"I'll live, boss."

I sat up and looked at Morrolan; he seemed even more exhausted than I. He was also very wet, as I was, and he was shivering as much as I, which I took a perverse pleasure in noting.

Presently he caught me looking at him. I suppose he guessed some of my thoughts, because he scowled at me. He sat up and I noticed his hands twitching as another scowl crossed his features. "Sorcery doesn't work here," he remarked. His voice sounded a bit odd, as if he was speaking through a very thin glass. Not really distant, yet not really close either. He said, "It would be nice to dry off."

"Not much wind, either," I said. "I guess we stay wet for a while." My voice sounded the same way, which I liked even less. I still felt cold, but it was warmer here than in the river.

"Let us proceed," said Morrolan.

"After you," I said.

We worked our way to our respective feet and looked around. The river behind us, corpses to the sides, and mists ahead.

"This place is weird, boss."

"I've noticed."

"Have you noticed that the corpses don't stink?"

"Yeah."

"Maybe it's the soul that gives off the stink, and since these guys don't have any soul, there isn't any smell."

I didn't ask Loiosh if he was serious, because I didn't want to know. Morrolan touched the hilt of his sword and checked to be sure the staff was still with him, reminding me of why we were here. He nodded to a direction off to his right. I girded my loins, so to speak, and we set off.

I sat in my favorite slouch-chair at home and considered how I was going to kill Kynn. What I wanted to do was just walk up and nail him, wherever he was; whoever was around. As I've said, this is not, in general, a bad policy. The trouble was that he knew there was a war going on, so he was being careful not to be alone.

I don't know how I got so fixed on Gruff's as the place

to nail him, and in thinking about the whole thing later I decided that had been a mistake and made sure to avoid such preconceptions. I knew I could take him in a public setting if I wanted to, because when I was a kid I'd seen someone assassinated in a public place—my father's restaurant. That was how I first met Kiera, too, but never mind that now.

I chewed the whole thing over for a while, until Loiosh said, *"Look, boss, if it's just a distraction you want, I can help."*

I said, *"Like hell you can."*

We were walking through swirling fog, which was merely annoying until I realized that there was no perceptible air movement to cause the fog to swirl. I pointed this out to Morrolan, who said, "Shut up."

I smiled, then smiled a little more as the end of a bare tree branch smacked him in the face. He deepened his scowl and we kept walking, albeit more slowly. Fog was the only thing to look at except the ground, which was soft and sandy and looked as if it couldn't contain growing things. As I'd reached this conclusion, a sudden shadow appeared before us which turned out to be a tree, as bare as the first.

"Boss, why are the trees bare in the summer?"

"You're asking me? Besides, if it were summer, it wouldn't be this chilly."

"Right."

More and more trees appeared as if they were sprouting in front of us, and we moved around them, keeping more or less to a single direction. Morrolan stopped shortly thereafter and studied what seemed to be a path running off diagonally to our left. His jaw worked and he said, "I don't think so. Let's keep going."

We did, and I said, "How can you tell?"

"The book."

"What book?"

"I was given a book to guide me through the Paths. Sethra helped, too."

"Who gave you the book?"

"It's a family inheritance."

"I see. How accurate is it?"

"We will find out, won't we? You may have been better off without me, for then Sethra would have been able to tell you of safer paths."

"Why couldn't she have told you the safer paths?"

"I am Dragaeran. I'm not allowed to know."

"Oh. Who makes up all these rules, anyway?"

He gave me one of his looks of disdain and no other answer. We came to another path leading off at a slightly different angle. Morrolan said, "Let's try this one."

I said, "You've memorized this book?"

He said, "Let us hope so."

The fog was thinner now, and I asked Morrolan if that was a good sign. He shrugged.

A bit later I said, "I take it there's a good reason for not bringing the book along."

He said, "It's not permitted."

"This whole trip isn't permitted, as I understand it."

"So why make things worse?"

I chewed that over and said, "Do you have any idea what's going to happen?"

"We will appear before the Lords of Judgment and ask them to restore my cousin."

"Do we have any good reasons why they should?"

"Our nerve for asking."

"Oh."

Shortly thereafter we came to a flat greyish stone set into the middle of the path. It was irregulary shaped, maybe two feet wide, four feet long, and sticking up about six inches out of the ground. Morrolan stopped and studied it for a moment, chewing his lip. I gave him silence to think for a while, then said, "Want to tell me about it?"

"It indicates a choice. Depending on which way we go around it, we will be taking a different way."

"What if we walk directly over it?"

He gave me a withering look and no other answer. Then he sighed and passed around the right side of it. I followed. The path continued among the naked trees, with no difference that I could detect.

Shortly thereafter we heard wolves howling. I looked at

Morrolan. He shrugged. "I'd rather deal with an external threat than an internal one at this point."

I decided not to ask what he meant. Loiosh shifted nervously on my shoulder. I said, "I'm getting the impression that these things have been set up deliberately, like a test or something."

He said, "Me, too."

"You don't know?"

"No."

More howling, and, *"Loiosh, can you tell how far away that was?"*

"Around here, boss? Ten feet or ten miles. Everything is weird. I'd feel better if I could smell something. This is scary."

"Feel like flying around for a look?"

"No. I'd get lost."

"Are you sure?"

"Yeah."

"Okay."

I caught a flicker of movement to my right and, as the adrenaline hit me, I realized that Morrolan had his sword out and that I did, too. Then there were greyish shapes appearing out of the mist and flying through the air at us, and there was a horrible moment of desperate action and it was over. I hadn't touched anything, and nothing had touched me.

Morrolan sighed and nodded. "They couldn't reach us," he said. "I'd hoped that was the case."

I sheathed my blade and wiped the sweat from my hands. I said, "If that's the worst we have to fear, I'll be fine." Loiosh came back out of my cloak.

Morrolan said, "Don't worry, it isn't."

Loiosh explained to me that he was now more than a year old. I allowed as to how this was true. He went on to say that he was damn near full grown, and ought to be allowed to help. I wondered in what way he could help. He suggested one. I couldn't think of a good counterargument, so there we were.

The next day, early, I returned to Gruff's. This time I

went inside and found an empty corner. I had a mug of honey-wine and left again. When I left, Loiosh wasn't with me.

I walked around to the back of the place and found the back door. It was locked. I played with it, then it was unlocked. I entered very carefully. It was a storeroom, filled with casks and barrels and boxes with bottles, and it could have kept me drunk for a year. Light crept past a curtain. So did I, finding myself in a room filled with glasses and plates and things one needs to wash dishes. I decided the area wasn't arranged very efficiently. I would have put the shelves to the left of the drying racks and . . . never mind.

There were no people in this room, either, but the low noise from the inn's main room came through the brown wool curtain. I remembered that curtain from the other side. I returned to the storeroom, moved two barrels and a large box, and hid myself.

Five aching, stiff, miserable hours later, Loiosh and I decided Kynn wasn't going to show up. If this continued, I was going to start taking a dislike to him. I massaged my legs until I could walk again, hoping no one would come through the door. Then I let myself out the back way, even managing to get the door locked behind me.

We were attacked twice more; once by something small and flying, and once by a tiassa. Neither of them could touch us, and both went away after one pass. We also came across several diverging or crossing paths, which Morrolan chose among with a confidence I hoped was justified.

We came to another grey stone, and Morrolan once more took the right-hand path, once again after some thought. I said, "Is it pretty much the way you remember it?" Morrolan didn't answer.

Then a thick old tree covered with knots appeared just off to our right, with a branch hanging across the path, about ten feet off the ground. A large brown bird that I recognized as an athyra studied us with one eye.

"You live," it said.

I said. *"How can you tell?"*

"You don't belong here."

"Oh. Well, I hadn't known that. We must have made a wrong turn on Undauntra. We'll just leave, then."

"You may not leave."

"Make up your mind. First you say—"

"Let's go, Vlad," said Morrolan. I assume that he was having his own little conversation with the athyra while I was having mine, but maybe not. We ducked under the branch and continued on our way. I looked back, but tree and bird were gone.

A little later Morrolan stood before another grey stone. This time he sighed, looked at me, and led us around to the left. He said, "We are going to have to, sooner or later, or we will never arrive at our destination."

"That sounds ominous."

"Yes."

And, a little later, "Can you give me a hint about what to expect?"

"No."

"Great."

And then I was falling. I started to scream, stopped, and realized that I was still walking next to Morrolan as before. I turned to him as I stumbled a bit. He stumbled at the same moment and his face turned white. He closed his eyes briefly and shook his head, looked at me, and continued down the path.

I said, "Were you falling there, just for a moment?"

"Falling? No."

"Then what happened to you?"

"Nothing I care to discuss."

I didn't press the issue.

A little later I took a step into quicksand. For a moment I thought it was going to be a repeat of the same kind of experience, because I was aware that, at the same time, I was still walking, but this time it didn't let up. Morrolan faltered next to me, then said, "Keep walking."

I did, though to one part of my mind it seemed that every step took me deeper. I also felt panic coming from Loiosh, which didn't help matters, as I wondered what he was seeing.

It occurred to me that Loiosh could feel my fear, too, so I tried to force myself to stay calm for his sake, telling myself that the quicksand was only an illusion. It must have worked, because I felt him calm down, and that helped me, and the image let up just as it was covering my mouth.

Morrolan and I stopped for a moment then, took a couple of deep breaths, and looked at each other. He shook his head once more.

I said, "Aren't there any clear paths to the Halls of Judgment?"

He said, "Some books have better paths than others."

I said, "When we get back, I'll steal one of the better ones and go into business selling copies."

"They can't be copied," said Morrolan. "There are those who have tried."

"How can that be? Words are words."

"I don't know. Let's continue."

We did, and I was quite relieved when we came to another grey stone and Morrolan took the right-hand path. This time it was a wild boar who couldn't touch us, and later a dzur.

Morrolan chose among more paths, and we came to another stone. He looked at me and said, "Well?"

I said, "If we have to."

He nodded and we went around it to the left.

I returned to my flat, my legs feeling better, my disposition sour. I decided I never wanted to see Gruff's again. I was beginning to get positively irritated at Kynn, who kept refusing to let himself be set up. I poured myself a glass of brandy and relaxed in my favorite chair, trying to think.

"So much for that idea, Loiosh."

"We could try it again tomorrow."

"My legs won't take it."

"Oh. What next, then?"

"Dunno. Let me think about it."

I paced my flat and considered options. I could purchase a sorcery spell of some sort, say, something that worked from a distance. But then someone would know I'd done it, and, furthermore, there are too many defenses against such things; I was even then wearing a ring that would block most attempts to use sorcery against me, and it had cost less than a week's pay. Witchcraft was too chancy and haphazard.

Poison? Once again, unreliable unless you're an expert. It was like dropping a rock on his head: It would probably work, but if it didn't he'd be alerted and it would be that much harder to kill him.

No, I was best off with a sword thrust; I could be certain what was going on. That meant I'd have to get close up behind him, or come on him unexpectedly. I drew my dagger from my belt and studied it. It was a knife-fighter's weapon; well made, heavy, with a reasonably good point and an edge that had been sharpened at about eight degrees. A chopping, slicing weapon that would work well against the back of a neck. My rapier was mostly point, suitable for coming up under the chin, and thus into the brain. Either would work.

I put the knife away again, squeezed my hands into fists, and paced a little more.

"Got something, boss?"

"I think so. Give me a minute to think about it."

"Okay."

And, a little later, *"All right, Loiosh, we're going to make this idiot-simple. Here's what I'll want you to do . . ."*

There were times when we were howling maniacs, times when we were hysterical with laughter.

Keep walking.

We were dying of hunger or thirst, with food or drink just to the side, off the path.

Keep walking.

Chasms opened before us, and the monsters of our nightmares bedeviled us, our friends turned against us, our enemies laughed in our faces. I guess I shouldn't speak for Morrolan, but the strained look of his back, the set of his jaw, and the paleness of his features spoke volumes.

Keep walking. If you stop, you'll never get out of it. If you leave the path you'll become lost. Walk into the wind, through the snowstorm, into the landslide. Keep walking.

Paths crisscrossing, Morrolan choosing, gritting our teeth

and going on. Hours? Minutes? Years? I dunno. And this despite the fact that anytime we took a right-hand path we were safe from the purely physical attacks. Once we were attacked by a phantom sjo-bear. I have a clear memory of it taking a swipe through my head and being amazed that I didn't feel it, but I still don't know if that was the product of a right-hand or a left-hand choice.

Frankly, I don't see how dead people manage it.

There came a point when we had to stop and rest and we did, taking food and drink, directly before another grey stone. I'd given up asking stupid questions. For one thing, I knew Morrolan wouldn't answer, and for another, I had the feeling that the next time he shrugged I was going to put a knife in his back. I suppose by that time he was feeling equally fond of me.

After a rest, then, we stood up again and Morrolan chose a left-hand path. I gritted my teeth.

"You holding up all right, Loiosh?"

"Just barely, boss. You?"

"About the same. I wish I knew how long this was going to go on. Or maybe I'm glad I don't."

"Yeah."

But, subjectively speaking, it wasn't long after that when the path before us suddenly widened. Morrolan stopped, looked up at me, and a faint smile lightened his features. He strode forward with renewed energy, and soon the trees were swallowed in mist, which cleared to reveal a high stone arch with a massive dragon's head carved into it. Our path led directly under the arch.

As we walked through it, Morrolan said, "The land of the dead."

I said, "I thought that's where we've been all along."

"No. That was the outlying area. Now things are likely to get strange."

12 –

I squeezed my right hand into a fist and slowly began to bring it toward my left. There was a resistance against my right hand that wasn't physical. It was as if I knew what I had to do, and wanted to do it, yet actually making the motion required fighting an incredible lassitude. I understood it—it was the resistance of the universe to being abused in this fashion—but that was of little help. Slowly, however, there was motion. I'd bring my hands together, and then the break would come, and I'd commit everything to it.

Failure was now, in a sense, impossible. My only options were success, or else madness and death.

My right fist touched my left hand.

A Dragaeran was approaching us at a nice, leisurely pace. His colors, black and silver, spoke of the House of the Dragon. He wore some sort of monster sword over his back. While we waited for him, I looked up at the sky, wondering whether it would be the typical orange-red overcast of the Dragaeran Empire. No, there wasn't any sky. A dull, uniform grey, with no break at all. Trying to figure out how high it was and what it was made me dizzy and queasy, so I stopped.

When the new arrival got close enough for me to see his face, his expression seemed not unpleasant. I don't think it could actually be friendly even if he wanted—not with a forehead that flat and lips as thin as paper. He came closer and I saw that he was breathing, and I couldn't decide whether to be surprised or not.

Then he stopped and his brow furrowed. He looked at me and said, "You're an Easterner." Then his gaze traveled to Morrolan and his eyes widened. "And you're living."

I said, "How can you tell?"

Morrolan snapped, "Shut up, Vlad." Then he inclined his head to the Dragonlord, saying, "We're on an errand."

"The living do not come here."

Morrolan said, "Zerika."

The Dragaeran's mouth twitched. "A Phoenix," he said. "And a special case."

"Nevertheless, we're here."

"You may have to bring your case to the Lords of Judgment."

"That," said Morrolan, "is what we came to do."

"And you will be required to prove yourselves."

"Of course," said Morrolan.

"Say what?" said I.

He turned a sneer toward me. "You will be required to face and defeat champions of—"

"This has got to be a joke," I said.

"Shut up, Vlad," said Morrolan.

I shook my head. "Why? Can you give me one good reason for making us fight our way to the Lords of Judgment, just so they can destroy us for being here?"

The stranger said, "We are of the House of the Dragon. We fight because we enjoy it." He gave me a nasty smile. turned, and walked away.

Morrolan and I looked at each other. He shrugged and I almost belted him. We looked around again, and we were surrounded by Dragonlords. I counted twelve of them. One of them took a step forward and said, "E'Baritt," and drew her sword.

Morrolan said, "E'Drien," and drew his. They saluted.

I backed away a step and said, "Are you sure we can touch them, and they us?"

"Yes," said Morrolan as he faced his opponent. "It wouldn't be fair otherwise."

"Oh. Of course. How silly of me."

They came within a few steps of each other, and Morrolan's opponent looked at the sword and licked her lips nervously.

"Don't worry," said Morrolan. "It does what I tell it to do."

The other nodded and took a sort of guard position, her left hand in front holding the dagger. Morrolan drew a dagger and matched her. He struck first with his sword, and she blocked it. She tried to strike with her dagger for his stomach, but he slipped around the blow and, pushing her off balance with his sword, struck her soundly in the chest with his dagger.

She bled. Morrolan stepped back and saluted.

After a moment I said to Morrolan, "Am I next, or are you doing all of them?"

One of the waiting Dragonlords said, "You're next, whiskers," as he stepped out, drew his sword, and faced me.

"Fine," I said, whipped out a throwing knife from my cloak, and threw it into his throat.

"Vlad!" called Morrolan.

"I've covered mine," I said, watching the guy writhe on the ground about six feet from Morrolan's victim. There came the sound of blades being drawn. Loiosh took off toward someone as I drew my rapier. It occurred to me that I might have committed some sort of social blunder.

Morrolan cursed and I heard the sound of steel on steel. Then there were two of them right in front of me. I feinted cuts toward their eyes, *flick flick,* spun to get a look at what was behind me, spun back, and threw three shuriken into the nearest stomach. Another Dragonlord almost took my head off, but then I sliced up his right arm bad enough that he couldn't hold his sword. He actually threatened me briefly with his dagger after that, which threat ended when my point took him cleanly through the chest, and that was it for the other one.

I had another throwing knife in my left hand by then, this one taken from the back of my collar. I used it to slow down the one nearest me, then charged another and veered off into a feint just outside of his sword range. His attack missed, then Loiosh flew into his face, then I cut open his chest and throat with my rapier.

I caught a glimpse of something moving, so I took a step to the side and lunged at it, then wondered if I were about to skewer Morrolan. But no, I skewered someone else instead, and was past him before he hit the ground. I got a glimpse of Morrolan fighting like a madman, then Loiosh screamed into my mind and I ducked and rolled as a sword passed over my head.

I came up, faced my enemy, feinted twice, then cut open her throat. Morrolan was dueling with a pair of them, and I thought about helping him, but then someone else was coming at me, and I don't remember how I dispatched him but I must have because I wasn't hurt.

I looked around for more targets but there weren't any; just the injured dead and the dead dead, so to speak. I wondered what happened to those who died here when they were already dead, as well as those who died here when they were alive.

Morrolan was glaring at me. I ignored him. I cleaned my rapier and sheathed it, trying to recover my breath. Loiosh returned to my shoulder, and I picked up my own belligerence reflected in his mind. Morrolan started to say something and I said, "Drop dead, asshole. You may think this multiple duel business is some sort of cute game, but I don't care to be tested. They wanted to kill me. They didn't manage. That's the end of it."

His face went white and he took a step toward me. "You never learn, do you?" He raised his sword until it was pointed at me.

I held my hand out. "Killing a man who isn't even holding a weapon? That would hardly be honorable, would it?"

He glared at me a moment longer, then spat on the ground. "Let's go," he said.

I left my various weapons in whatever bodies they hap-

pened to have taken up residence and followed him farther
into the land of the dead.

I hoped the rest of the dead we met would be more
peaceful.

There are times, I guess, when you have to trust some-
body. I would have chosen Kiera, but I didn't know where
she was. So I gave Kragar some money and had him purchase, discreetly, a seven-inch blade. It took
him an afternoon, and he didn't ask any questions.

I tested the balance and decided I liked it. I spent an hour
in my flat sharpening the point. I shouldn't have taken an
hour, but I was used to sharpening edges for vegetables or
meat, not sharpening points for bodies. It's a different skill.
After sharpening it, I decided to put a coat of dull black
paint on the blade and, after some thought, on the hilt, too.
I left the actual edge of the blade unpainted.

When I was done it was already evening. I went back to
Gruff's and positioned Loiosh in the window of the place.
I took up a position around the corner and waited.

"Well, Loiosh? Is he there?"

"Ummm . . . yeah. I see him, boss."

"Is he with his friend?"

"Yeah. And a couple of others."

"Are you sure you're out of sight?"

"Don't worry about it, boss."

"Okay. We'll wait, then."

I went over my plan, such as it was, a couple of times
in my head, then settled back to do some serious waiting.
I amused myself by thinking up fragments of bad poetry
for a while, which put me in mind of an Eastern girl named
Sheila whom I'd gone out with for a few months a year
before. She was from South Adrilankha, where most humans
live, and I guess she was attracted to me because I had
money and seemed tough. I suppose I *am* tough, come to
think of it.

Anyway, she was good for me, even though it didn't last
long. She wanted to be rich, and classy, and she was an
argumentative bitch. I was working on keeping my mouth

shut when Dragaeran punks insulted me, and she helped a lot because the only way to get along with her was to bite my tongue when she made her outrageous statements about Dragaerans or the Jhereg or whatever. We'd had a lot of fun for a while, but she finally caught a ship to one of the island duchies where they paid well for human singers. I missed her, but not a lot.

Thinking about her and our six-hour shopping sprees when I had money was a good way to waste time. I went through the list of names we'd called each other one afternoon when we were trying to see who could get cute enough to make the other ill. I was actually starting to get melancholy and teary-eyed when Loiosh said, *"They're leaving, boss."*

"Okay. Back here."

He came back to my shoulder. I stuck my head around the corner. It was very dark, but in the light escaping from the inn I could see them. It certainly was my target. He was walking right toward me. As I ducked back behind the building, my heart gave one quick thud, there was a drop in my stomach, and I felt I was perspiring, just for an instant. Then I was cool and relaxed, my mind clear and sharp. I took the stiletto from its sheath at my side.

"Go, Loiosh. Be careful."

He left my shoulder. I adjusted the weapon to an overhand grip because Dragaerans are taller than we are. Eye level for Kynn was just a bit over my head. No problem.

Then I heard, "What the— Get that thing away from me!" At the same time, there was laughter. I guess Kynn was amused by his friend's dance with a jhereg. I stepped around the corner. I can't tell you what Loiosh was doing to Kynn's friend because I had eyes only for my target. His back was to me, but he turned quickly as I emerged from the alley.

His eyes were on a level with the blade, but the knife and my sleeve were dark, so his eyes locked with my own, in the tiny instant when the world froze around me and all motion slowed down. He appeared slightly startled.

It wasn't as if I hesitated. The motion of my knife was mechanical, precise, and irresistible. He had no time to register the threat before the stiletto took him in the left eye. He gave a jerk and a gasp as I twisted the knife once to be sure. I left it in him and stepped back into the alley as I heard his body fall. I crouched between two garbage cans and waited.

Then I heard cursing from around the corner.

"I'm away, boss, and he's found the body."

"Okay, Loiosh. Wait."

I saw the guy come around the corner, sword out, looking. By this time I had another knife in my hand. But I was hoping that, knowing there was an assassin around, the guy wouldn't be interested in looking too closely for him. I was right, too. He just gave a cursory glance up the alley, then probably decided that I'd teleported away.

He took off at a run, probably to inform his boss of what had happened. As soon as Loiosh told me it was safe, I continued through the alley and, walking quickly but not running, made my way back to my flat. By the time I arrived I wasn't trembling anymore. Loiosh joined me before I got there. I stripped off all of my clothing and checked for bloodstains. My jerkin was stained, so I burned it in the kitchen stove. Then I bathed, while thinking about how to spend my money.

Our friend from the gate—the Dragonlord with the flat forehead—joined us again. He glared at me and I sneered back. Loiosh hissed at him, which I think unnerved him just a bit. We won the exchange, though it was close. He turned to Morrolan, who actually seemed a little embarrassed. Morrolan said, "My companion—"

"Do not speak of it," said the other.

"Very well."

"Follow."

Morrolan shot me one more glare for good luck and we set off behind him. The area seemed empty of trees, rocks, or buildings. Every once in a while, off in the distance, we would see figures moving. As I continued looking, trying to avoid looking at the sky, it seemed that things were shifting a bit, as if our steps were taking us over more ground than just a footstep ought to, and the position of landmarks would change out of proportion to our rate of movement. Well, this shouldn't surprise me. I went back to concentrating on our friend's back.

Then someone else came toward us—a woman dressed in a robe of bright purple. Our guide stopped and spoke quietly to her, and she turned and went off again.

"Boss, did you get a look at her eyes?"

"No, I didn't notice. What about them?"

"They were empty, boss. Nothing. Like, no brain or something."

"Interesting."

The landscape began changing. I can't be precise about when or to what, because I was trying not to watch. The changes didn't make sense with how we were moving, and I didn't like it. It was almost like a short teleport, except I didn't get sick or feel any of the effects. I saw a grove of pine trees and then they vanished; there was a very large boulder, big and dark grey, directly in front of us, but it was gone as we started to step around it. I'm sure there were mountains not too far away at one point, and that we were walking through a jungle at another, and next to an ocean somewhere in there. In a way, this was more disconcerting than the attacks we'd endured earlier.

It started raining just as I was getting dry again after the soaking we'd started this journey with. I hate being wet.

The rain lasted only long enough to annoy me, then we were walking among sharp, jutting rocks. Our path seemed to have been cut through the stonework, and I'd have guessed we were in a mountain.

It was then that a dragon appeared before us.

I ran into Kragar the next day. He cleared his throat and looked away in the particular way he has and said, "I heard that one of Rolaan's enforcers went for a walk last night."

I said, "Yeah?"

He said, "No one saw who did it, but I heard a rumor that the assassin used a jhereg to distract the guy he was with."

I said, "Oh."

He said, "I'd almost think of you, Vlad, except you're so well known for having a pet jhereg that you couldn't possibly be stupid enough to do something that obvious."

I suddenly felt queasy. Loiosh said, *"Pet?"*

I said, *"Shut up,"* to Loiosh, and "that's true," to Kragar.

He nodded. "It was interesting, though."

I said, "Yeah."

My boss sent for me a little later. He said, "Vlad, you should leave town for a while. Probably a month. You have anywhere to go?"

I said, "No."

He handed me another bag of gold. "Find somewhere you'll like. It's on me. Enjoy yourself and stay out of sight."

I said, "Okay. Thanks." I got out of there and found a commercial sorcerer with no Jhereg connections to teleport me to Candletown, which is along the seacoast to the east and is known for food and entertainments. I didn't even stop home first. It didn't seem wise.

It is really hard to conceive of just how big a dragon is. I can tell you that it could eat me, perhaps without the need for a second bite. I can mention that it has tentaclelike things all around its head, each of which is longer than I am tall and as big around as my thigh. I could let you know that, at the shoulders, it was around eighteen feet high and much, much longer than that. But, until you've seen one up close, you just can't really imagine it.

Loiosh dived under my cloak. I'd have liked to have followed. Morrolan stood stiffly at my side, waiting. His hand wasn't resting on his sword hilt, so I kept my hands away from my rapier.

Anyway, just what good is a rapier going to do against a dragon?

"WELL MET, STRANGERS."

What can I say? It wasn't "loud" as a voice is loud, but, ye gods, I felt the insides of my skull pounding. Earlier, when the athyra had spoken to us, I had the impression that it was carrying on simultaneous but different conversations with Morrolan and me. This time, it seemed, we were both in on it. If I ever actually come to understand psychic communication I'll probably go nuts.

Morrolan said, *"Well met, dragon."*

One of its eyes was fixed on me, the other, I assume, on Morrolan.

It said, *"YOU ARE ALIVE."*

I said, *"How can you tell?"*

Morrolan said, *"We are on an errand."*

"FOR WHOM?"

"The lady Aliera, of the House of the Dragon."

"OF WHAT IMPORTANCE IS THIS TO ME?"

"I don't know. Does the House of the Dragon matter to you, Lord Dragon?"

I heard what may have been a chuckle. It said, *"YES."*

Morrolan said, *"Aliera e'Kieron is the Dragon heir to the throne."*

That was news to me. I stared at Morrolan while I wondered at the ramifications of this.

The dragon turned its head so both its eyes were on Morrolan. After a moment it said, *"WHERE STANDS THE CYCLE?"*

Morrolan said, *"It is the reign of the Phoenix."*

The dragon said, *"YOU MAY BOTH PASS."*

It turned around (not a minor undertaking) and walked back out of sight. I relaxed. Loiosh emerged from my cloak and took his place on my right shoulder.

Our guide continued to lead us onward, and soon we were back in a more normal (ha!) landscape. I wondered how much time had actually passed for us since we'd arrived. Our clothing had pretty much dried before the rain and we'd had a meal. Four hours? Six?

There was a building ahead of us, and there seemed to be more people around, some in the colors of the House of the Dragon, others in purple robes.

"Morrolan, do you know the significance of those dressed in purple?"

"They are the servants of the dead."

"Oh. Bitch of a job."

"It is what happens to those who arrive in the Paths of the Dead but don't make it through, or who die here."

I shuddered, thinking of the Dragonlords we'd killed. "Is it permanent?"

"I don't think so. It may last for a few thousand years, though."

I shuddered again. "It must get old, fast."

"I imagine. It is also used as punishment. It is likely what will happen to us if our mission fails."

The building was still quite some distance in front of us, but I could see that it would have compared well to the Imperial Palace. It was a simple, massive cube, all grey, with no markings or decorations I could distinguish. It was ugly.

Our guide gestured toward it and said, "The Halls of Judgment."

13 –

I held the world in my hands. There was a moment of incredible clarity, when the horizon stopped wavering, and I was deaf to rhythms and pulses. Everything held its breath, and my thought pierced the fabric of reality. I felt Loiosh's mind together with mine as a perfectly tuned lant, and I realized that, except for my grandfather, he was the only being in the world that I loved.

Why was I doing this?

The scent of pine needles penetrated my thoughts, and everything seemed clean and fresh. It brought tears to my eyes and power to my hands.

As we approached the building, it didn't get any smaller. I think the area around me continued to change, but I wasn't noticing. We came to an arch with another stylized dragon's head, and our guide stopped there. He bowed to Morrolan, studiously ignoring me. I said, "It's been a pleasure. Have a wonderful time here."

His eyes flicked over me and he said, "May you be granted a purple robe."

"Why, thanks," I said. "You, too."

We passed beneath the arch. We were in a sort of courtyard in front of doors I suspect our friend the dragon could have gone through without ducking. I saw other arches leading into it, about twenty of them.

Oh. No, of course. Make that exactly seventeen of them. There were several purple robes standing around in the courtyard, one of whom was approaching us. He made no comment, only bowed to us both, turned, and led us toward the doors.

It was a long way across the courtyard. I had a chance to think about all sorts of possibilities I didn't enjoy contemplating. When we were before the doors they slowly and majestically swung open for us, with an assumed grandeur that seemed to work on me even though I was aware of it.

"Stole one of your tricks," I told Morrolan.

"It is effective, is it not?"

"Yeah."

Back when the doors of Castle Black had opened, Lady Teldra had stood there to greet me. When the doors of the Halls of Judgment opened before us, there was a tall male Dragaeran in the dress of the House of the Lyorn—brown ankle-length skirt, doublet, and sandals—with a sword slung over his back.

He saw me and his eyes narrowed. Then he looked at the pair of us and they widened. "You are living men."

I said, "How could you tell?"

"Good Lyorn," said Morrolan, "we wish to present ourselves to the Lords of Judgment."

He sort of smiled. "Yes, I suppose you do. Very well, follow me. I will present you at once."

"I can hardly wait," I muttered. No one responded.

I spent the two weeks following Kynn's death in Candletown, discovering just how much fun you can have while you're worried sick; or, if you wish, just how miserable you can be while you're living it up.

Then, one day while I was sitting on the beach quietly getting drunk, a waiter came up to me and said, "Lord Mawdyear?" I nodded, as that was close enough to the name

I was using. He handed me a sealed message for which I tipped him lavishly. It read "Come back," and my boss had signed it. I spent a few minutes wondering if it was faked, until Loiosh pointed out that anyone who knew enough to fake it knew enough to send someone to kill me right there on the beach. This sent a chill through me, but it also convinced me the message was genuine.

I teleported back the next morning, and nothing was said about what I thought must have been a miserable blunder. I found out, over the course of the next few months, that it hadn't really been that bad a mistake. It was pretty much the policy to send the assassin out of town after he shined someone, especially during a war. I also found out that going to Candletown was a cliché; it was sometimes referred to as Killertown. I never went back there.

But there was something I noticed right away, and I still don't really understand it. My boss knew I'd killed the guy, and Kragar certainly guessed it, but I don't think many others even suspected. Okay, then why did everyone treat me differently?

No, it wasn't big things, but just the way people I worked with would look at me; it was like I was a different person— someone worthy of respect, someone to be careful of.

Mind you, I'm not complaining; it was a great feeling. But it puzzled me then and it still does. I can't figure out if rumors got around, or if my behavior changed in some subtle way. Probably a little of each.

But you know what was even more strange? As I would meet other enforcers who worked for someone or other in the strange world of the Jhereg, I would, from time to time, look at one and say to myself, "That one's done 'work.' " I have no idea how I knew, and I guess I can't even guarantee I was right, but I felt it. And, more often than not, the guy would look at me and give a kind of half nod as if he recognized something about me, too.

I was seventeen years old, a human in the Dragaeran Empire, and I'd taken a lot of garbage over the years. Now I was no longer an "Easterner," nor was I Dragaeran or even a Jhereg. Now I was someone who could calmly and coldly end a life, and then go out and spend the money, and I wasn't going to have to take any crap anymore.

Which was a nice feeling while it lasted.

I wondered, walking through the Halls, if there were ever any dragons brought there for judgment. I mean, not only were the doors large enough to admit one, but the halls were, too. At any rate, the scale made me feel small and insignificant, which was probably the reason behind the whole thing.

Reason?

"*Loiosh, who designed this place, anyway?*"

"*You're asking me, boss? I don't know. The gods, I suppose.*"

"*And if I just knew what that meant, I'd be fine.*"

"*Have you noticed that there isn't any decoration? Nothing at all.*"

"*Hmmm. You're right, Loiosh. But, on the other hand, what sort of mood would you pick if you were decorating this place?*"

"*A point.*"

The place was nearly empty, save for a few purple robes coming or going, all with that same blank look. Seeing them made me queasy. I didn't notice any side passages or doors, but I don't think I was at my most observant. It was big and it was impressive. What can I say?

"Good day," said someone behind us. We turned and saw a male Dragaeran in the full splendor of a Dragonlord wizard, complete with shining black and silver garb and a staff that was taller than he was. His smile was sardonic as he looked at Morrolan. I turned to see my companion's expression. His eyes were wide. I'd now seen Morrolan wet, embarrassed, and startled. If I could just see him frightened, my life would be complete.

I said, "Are you certain it's day?"

He turned his sardonic expression to me and sent me the most withering glare I've ever experienced. Several comments came to mind, but for once I couldn't manage to get them out. This may have saved my life.

Morrolan said, "I salute you, Lord Baritt. I had thought you were yet living. I grieve to know—"

He snorted. "Time flows differently here. Doubtless when you left, I hadn't been . . . ." He scowled and didn't complete the sentence.

Morrolan indicated the surrounding wall. "You live within this building, Lord?"

"No, I merely do research here."

"Research?"

"I suppose you wouldn't be familiar with the concept."

By this time I'd recovered enough to appreciate someone being contemptuous of Morrolan. Morrolan, on the other hand, didn't appreciate it at all. He drew himself up and said, "My lord, if I have done something to offend you—"

"I can't say much for your choice of traveling companions."

Before Morrolan could respond, I said, "I don't like it either, but—"

"Don't speak in my presence," said Baritt. As he said it, I found that I couldn't; my mouth felt like it was filled with a whole pear, and I discovered that I couldn't breathe. I hadn't thought it possible to perform sorcery here. The Lyorn who was guiding me took a step forward, but at that moment I found I could breathe again. Baritt said "Jhereg" as if it were a curse. Then he spat on the floor in front of me and stalked away.

When he was gone I took a couple of deep breaths and said, "Hey, and here I'd thought he hated me because I'm an Easterner."

Morrolan had no witty rejoinder for that. Our guide inclined his head slightly, from which I deduced that we were to follow him. We did.

A few minutes later he had led us to a big square entrance way, which was where the hall ended. He stopped outside it and indicated that we should continue through. We bowed to him and stepped forward into another world.

After Kynn's death, and its aftermath, I learned slowly. I trained in sorcery in hopes of being able to follow someone teleporting, but that turned out to be even harder than I'd thought.

I never again used Loiosh as a distraction, but he got better at other things, such as observing a target for me and making sure an area was free of Phoenix Guards or other annoyances.

The war between Rolaan and Welok lasted for several months, during which everyone was careful and didn't go out alone. This was an education for me. I "worked" several more times during that period, although only once was it a direct part of the war as far as I know.

The mystery, though, is where, by all the gods, my money went. I ought to have been rich. The fee for assassination is high. I was now living in a nice comfortable flat (it was *really* nice—it had this great blue and white carpet and a huge kitchen with a built-in wood stove), but it didn't cost all that much. I was eating well, and paying quite a bit for sorcery lessons, as well as paying a top fencing master, but none of these things comes close to accounting for all the income I was generating. I don't gamble a whole lot, which is a favorite means of losing money for many Jhereg. I just can't figure it out.

Of course, some of it I can trace. Like, I met an Eastern girl named Jeanine, and we hung out together for most of a year, and it's amazing how much you can spend on entertainment if you really put your mind to it. And there was a period when I was paying out a lot for teleports—like two or three a day for a couple of weeks. That was when I was seeing Jeanine and Constance at the same time and I didn't want them finding out about each other. It ended because all the teleports were making me too sick to be of much good to either of them. I guess, in retrospect, that could account for quite a bit of the money, couldn't it? Teleports don't come cheap.

Still, I can't figure it out. It doesn't really matter, I suppose.

My first reaction was that we'd stepped outside, and in a way I was right, but it was no outside I'd ever seen before. There were stars, such as my grandfather had shown me, and they were bright and hard, all over the place, and so *many* of them. . . .

Presently I realized that my neck was hurting and that

the air was cold. Morrolan, next to me, was still gawking at the stars. I said, "Morrolan."

He said, "I'd forgotten what they were like." Then he shook his head and looked around. I did the same at just about the same time, and we saw, seated on thrones, the Lords of Judgment.

Two of them were right in front of us; others were off to the sides, forming what may have been a massive circle of thrones, chairs, and like that. Some of them were grouped close together, in pairs or trios, while others seemed all alone. The creature directly before me, perhaps fifty feet away, was huge and green. Morrolan began walking toward it. As we came closer, I saw that it was covered with scalelike hide, and its eyes were huge and deep-set. I recognized this being as Barlan, and an urge to prostrate myself came over me; I still have no idea why. I resisted.

Next to him was one who looked like a Dragaeran, dressed in a gown of shifting colors, with a haughty face and hair like fine mist. I looked at her hands, and, yes, each finger had an extra joint. Here was the Demon Goddess of my ancestors, Verra. I looked to her right, half expecting to see the sisters legends claimed she had. I think I saw them, too—one was small and always in shadow, and next to her was one whose skin and hair flowed like water. I avoided looking at either of them. I controlled my shaking and forced myself to follow Morrolan.

There were others, but I hardly remember them, save one who seemed to be dressed in fire, and another who seemed always to be fading into and out of existence. How many? I can't say. I remember the few I've mentioned, and I know there were others. I retain the impression that there were thousands of them, perhaps millions, but you'll forgive me if I don't trust my senses fully.

Morrolan seemed to be steering us to a point between Verra and Barlan. As we neared them, it seemed that their gigantic size was illusory. We stopped when we were perhaps fifteen feet from them, and they appeared large, but hardly inhuman. At least in size. Barlan was covered with green scales and had those frightening huge pale green eyes. And Verra's hair still shimmered, and her clothing refused to stop changing color, form, and material. Nevertheless, they seemed more like beings I might be able to talk to than some of the others in the area.

They acknowledged us at the same moment.

Morrolan bowed, but not as low as he had to Baritt. I didn't try to figure it out; I just bowed myself, very low indeed. Verra looked back and forth between the two of us, then over at Barlan. She seemed to be smiling. I couldn't tell about him.

Then she looked back at us. Her voice, when she spoke, was deep and resonating, and very odd. It was as if her words would echo in my mind, only there was no gap in time between hearing them in my mind and in my ears. The result was an unnatural sort of piercing clarity to everything she said. It was such a strange phenomenon that I had to stop and remember her words, which were: "This is a surprise."

Barlan said nothing. Verra turned to him, then back to us. "What are your names?"

Morrolan said, "I am Morrolan e'Drien, Duke of the House of the Dragon."

I swallowed and said, "Vladimir Taltos, Baronet of the House of the Jhereg."

"Well, well, well," said Verra. Her smile was strange and twisted and full of irony. She said, "It would seem that you are both alive."

I said, "How could you tell?"

Her smile grew a bit wider. She said, "When you've been in the business as long as I have—"

Barlan spoke, saying, "State your errand."

"We have come to beg for a life."

Verra's eyebrows went up. "Indeed? For whom?"

"My cousin," said Morrolan, indicating the staff.

Barlan held his hand out, and Morrolan stepped forward and gave him the staff. Morrolan stepped back.

"You must care for her a great deal," said Verra, "since by coming here you have forfeited your right to return."

I swallowed again. I think Verra noticed this, because she looked at me and said, "Your case is less clear, as Easterners do not belong here at all."

I licked my lips and refrained from comment.

Verra turned back to Morrolan and said, "Well?"

"Yes?"

"Is she worth your life?"

Morrolan said, "It is necessary. Her name is Aliera e'Kieron, and she is the Dragon heir to the throne."

Verra's head snapped back, and she stared straight into Morrolan's face. There is something terrifying about seeing a god shocked.

After a little while, Verra said, "So, she has been found."

Morrolan nodded.

Verra gestured toward me. "Is that where the Easterner comes in?"

"He was involved in recovering her."

"I see."

"Now that she has been found, we ask that she be allowed to resume her life at the point where—"

"Spare me the details," said Verra. Morrolan shut up.

Barlan said, "What you ask is impossible."

Verra said, "Is it?"

"It is also forbidden," said Barlan.

"Tough cookies," said Verra.

Barlan said, "By our positions here we have certain responsibilities. One of them is to uphold—"

"Spare me the lecture," said Verra. "You know who Aliera is."

"If she is sufficiently important, we may ask to convene—"

"By which time the Easterner will have been here too long to return. And his little jhereg, too." I hardly reacted to this at the time, because I was too amazed by the spectacle of the gods arguing. But I did notice it, and I noted that Verra was aware of Loiosh even though my familiar was inside my cloak.

Barlan said, "That is not our concern."

Verra said, "A convocation will also be boring."

"You would break our trust to avoid boredom?"

"You damn betcha, feather-breath."

Barlan stood. Verra stood. They glared at each other for

a moment, then vanished in a shower of golden sparks.

It is not only the case that Dragaerans have never learned to cook; it is also true, and far more surprising, that most of them will admit it. That is why Eastern restaurants are so popular, and the best of them is Valabar's.

Valabar and Sons has existed for an impossibly long time. It was here in Adrilankha before the Interregnum made this city the Imperial Capital. That's hundreds of years, run by the same family. The same family of humans. It was, according to all reports, the first actual restaurant within the Empire; the first place that existed as a business just to serve meals, rather than a tavern that had food, or a hotel that supplied board for a fee.

There must be some sort of unwritten law about the place that those in power know, something that says, "Whatever we're going to do to Easterners, leave Valabar's alone." It's that good.

It is a very simple place on the inside, with white linen tablecloths and simple furnishings, but none of the decoration that most places have. The waiters are pleasant and charming and very efficient, and almost as difficult to notice as Kragar when they are slipping up on you to refill your wine glass.

They have no menus; instead your waiter stands there and recites the list of what the chef, always called "Mr. Valabar" no matter how many Valabars are working there at the moment, is willing to prepare today.

My date for the evening, Mara, was the most gorgeous blonde I'd ever met, with a rather nasty wit that I enjoyed when it wasn't turned on me. Kragar's date was a Dragaeran lady whose name I can't remember, but whose House was Jhereg. She was one of the tags in a local brothel, and she had a nice laugh.

The appetizer of the day was anise-jelled winneoceros cubes, the soup was a very spicy potato soup with Eastern red pepper, the sorbet was lemon, the pâté—made of goose liver, chicken liver, kethna liver, herbs, and unsalted butter—was served on hard-crusted bread with cucumber slices that had been just barely pickled. The salad was served with an impossibly delicate vinegar dressing that was almost sweet but not quite.

Kragar had fresh scallops in lemon and garlic sauce, Kragar's date had the biggest stuffed cabbage in the world, Mara had duck in plum brandy sauce, and I had kethna in Eastern red pepper sauce. We followed it with dessert pancakes, mine with finely ground walnuts and cream chocolate brandy sauce topped with oranges. We also had a bottle of Piarran Mist, the Fenarian dessert wine. I paid for the whole thing, because I'd just killed someone.

We were all feeling giggly as we walked the meal off; then Mara and I went up to my flat and I discovered that a meal at Valabar's is one of the world's great aphrodisiacs. I wondered what my grandfather would make of that information.

Mara got tired of me and dumped me a week or so later, but what the hell.

I said, "Feather-breath?"

Loiosh said, *"Sheesh."*

"I think," said Morrolan judiciously, "that we've managed to get someone in trouble."

"Yeah."

Morrolan looked around, as did I. None of the other beings present seemed to be paying us any attention. We were still standing there a few minutes later when Verra reappeared in another shower of sparks. She had a gleam in her eye. Barlan appeared then, and, as before, his expression was unreadable. I noticed then that Verra was holding the staff.

Verra said, "Come with me."

She stepped down from her throne and led us around behind it, off into the darkness. She didn't speak and Morrolan didn't speak. I certainly wasn't going to say anything. Loiosh was under my cloak again.

We came to a place where there was a very high wall. We walked along it for a moment, passing another purple robe or two, until we came to a high arch. We passed beneath it, and there were two corridors branching away.

Verra took the one to the right and we followed. In a short time, it opened to a place where a wide, shallow brick well stood, making water noises.

Verra dipped her hand into the well and took a drink; then, with no warning, she smashed the staff into the side of the well.

There was the requisite cracking sound, then I was blinded by a flash of pure white light, and I think the ground trembled. When I was able to open my eyes again, there was still some sort of visual distortion, as if the entire area we were in had been bent at some impossible angle, and only Verra could be seen clearly.

Things settled down then, and I saw what appeared to be the body of a female Dragaeran in the black and silver of the House of the Dragon stretched out next to the well. I noticed at once that her hair was blonde—even more rare in a Dragonlord than in a human. Her brows were thin, and the slant of her closed eyes was rather attractive. I think a Dragaeran would have found her *very* attractive. Verra dipped her hand in again and allowed some of the water to flow into the mouth of her whom I took to be Aliera.

Then Verra smiled at us and walked away.

Aliera began to breathe.

14 –

My grandfather, in teaching me fencing, used to make me stand for minutes at a time, watching for the movement of his blade that would give me an opening. I suspect that he knew full well that he was teaching me more than fencing.

When the moment came, I was ready.

Her eyes fluttered open, but she didn't focus on anything. I decided that she was better looking alive than she'd been dead. Morrolan and I stood there for a moment, then he said softly, "Aliera?"

Her eyes snapped to him. There was a pause before her face responded; when it did she seemed puzzled. She started to speak, stopped, cleared her throat, and croaked, "Who are you?"

He said, "I'm your cousin. My name is Morrolan e'Drien. I am the eldest son of your father's youngest sister."

"Morrolan," she repeated. "Yes. That would be the right sort of name." She nodded as if he'd passed a test. I took in Morrolan's face, but he seemed to be keeping any expression off it. Aliera tried to sit up, failed, and her eyes fell

144

on me; narrowed. She turned to Morrolan and said, "Help me."

He helped her to sit up. She looked around. "Where am I?"

"The Halls of Judgment," said Morrolan.

Surprise. "I'm dead?"

"Not anymore."

"But—"

"I'll explain," said Morrolan.

"Do so," said Aliera.

"Those two must be related," I told Loiosh. He sniggered.

"What is the last thing you remember?"

She shrugged, a kind of one-shoulder-and-tilt-of-the-head thing that was almost identical to Morrolan's. "It's hard to say." She closed her eyes. We didn't say anything. A moment later she said. "There was a strange whining sound, almost above my audible range. Then the floor shook, and the ceiling and walls started to buckle. And it was becoming very hot. I was going to teleport out, and I remember thinking that I couldn't do it fast enough, and then I saw Sethra's face." She paused, looking at Morrolan. "Sethra Lavode. Do you know her?"

"Rather," said Morrolan.

Aliera nodded. "I saw her face, then I was running through a tunnel—I think that was a dream. It lasted a long time, though. Eventually I stopped running and lay on what seemed to be a white tile floor, and I couldn't move and didn't want to. I don't know how long I was there. Then someone shouted my name—I thought at the time it was my mother. Then I was waking up, and I heard a strange voice calling my name. I think that was you, Morrolan, because then I opened my eyes and saw you."

Morrolan nodded. "You have been asleep—dead, actually—for, well, several hundred years."

Aliera nodded, and I saw a tear in her eye. She said very quietly, "It is the reign of a reborn Phoenix, isn't it?"

Morrolan nodded, seeming to understand.

"I told him it would be," she said. "A Great Cycle—seventeen Cycles; it had to be a reborn Phoenix. He wouldn't listen to me. He thought it was the end of the Cycle, that a new one could be formed. He—"

"He created a sea of chaos, Aliera."

"What?"

I decided that "he" referred to Adron. I doubted that he was to be found in these regions.

"Not as big as the original, perhaps, but it is there—where Dragaera City used to be."

"Used to be," she echoed.

"The capital of the Empire is now Adrilankha."

"Adrilankha. A seacoast town, right? Isn't that where Kieron's Tower is?"

"Kieron's Watch. It used to be there. It fell into the sea during the Interregnum."

"Inter— Oh. Of course. How did it end?"

"Zerika, of the House of the Phoenix, retrieved the Orb, which somehow landed here, in the Paths of the Dead. She was allowed to return with it. I helped her," he added.

"I see," she said. Morrolan sat down next to her. I sat down next to Morrolan. Aliera said, "I don't know Zerika."

"She was not yet born. She's the only daughter of Vernoi and, um, whoever it was she married."

"Loudin."

"Right. They both died in the Disaster."

She nodded, then stopped. "Wait. If they both died in the explosion, and Zerika wasn't born when it happened, how could . . . ?"

Morrolan shrugged. "Sethra had something to do with it. I've asked her to explain it, but she just looks smug." He blinked. "I get the impression that, whatever it was she did, she was too busy doing it to rescue you as thoroughly as she'd have liked. I guess you were the second priority after making sure there could be an Emperor. Zerika is the last Phoenix."

"The last Phoenix? There can't be another? Then the Cycle is broken. If not now, for the future."

"Maybe," said Morrolan.

"Can there be another Phoenix?"

"How should I know? We have the whole Cycle to worry about it. Ask me again in a few hundred thousand years when it starts to matter."

I could see from Aliera's expression that she didn't like

this answer, but she didn't respond to it. There was a silence, then she said, "What happened to me?"

"I don't understand entirely," said Morrolan. "Sethra managed to preserve your soul in some form, though it became lost. Eventually—I imagine shortly after Zerika took the Orb—an Athyra wizard found you. He was studying necromancy. I don't think he realized what he had. You were tracked down, and—"

"Who tracked me down?"

"Sethra and I," he said, watching her face. He glanced at me quickly, then said, "And there were others who helped, some time ago."

Aliera closed her eyes and nodded. I hate it when they talk over my head. "Did you have any trouble getting me back?"

Morrolan and I looked at each other. "None to speak of," I said.

Aliera looked at me, then looked again, her eyes narrow. She stared hard, as if she were looking inside of me. She said, "Who *are* you?"

"Vladimir Taltos, Baronet, House Jhereg."

She stared a little longer, then shook her head and looked back at Morrolan.

"What is it?" he asked.

"Never mind." She stood up suddenly, or, rather, tried, then sat down. She scowled. "I want to get out of here."

"I believe they will let Vlad leave. If so, he will help you."

She looked at me, then back at Morrolan. "What's wrong with you?"

"As a living man, I am not allowed to return from the Paths of the Dead. I shall remain here."

Aliera stared at him. "Like hell you will. I'll see you dead first."

It's hard for me to pin down the point at which I stopped considering myself to be someone's enforcer who sometimes did "work" and started considering myself a free-lance assassin. Part of it was that I worked for several different people during a short period of time during and after the war, including Welok himself, so this made things confusing.

Certainly those around me began to think of me that way before it occurred to me, but I don't think my own thinking changed until I had developed professional habits and a good approach to the job.

Once again, it's unclear just when this occurred, but I was certainly functioning like a professional by the time I finished my seventh job—assassinating a little turd named Raiet.

While I was thinking over this announcement and wondering whether to laugh, I realized that Verra had left us; in other words, we had no way of knowing where to go from here.

I cleared my throat. Morrolan broke off from his staring contest with Aliera and said, "Yes, Vlad?"

"Do you know how we can find our way back to where all the gods were?"

"Hmmm. I think so."

"Let's do that, then."

"Why?"

"Do you have a better idea?"

"I suppose not."

As I stood, I was taken with a fleeting temptation to take a drink from the well. It's probably fortunate that it was only fleeting. We helped Aliera to stand, and I discovered that she was quite short—hardly taller than me, as a matter of fact.

We began walking back the way we'd come, Morrolan and me each supporting one of Aliera's arms. She looked very unhappy. Her teeth were clenched, perhaps from anger, perhaps from pain. Her eyes, which I'd first thought were green, seemed to be grey, and were set straight ahead.

We made it back to the archway and rested there for a moment.

Morrolan suggested that Aliera sit down and rest her legs. Aliera said, "Shut up."

I saw that Morrolan's patience was wearing thin. So was mine, for that matter. We bit our lips at the same moment, caught each other's eyes, and smiled a little.

We took her arms and started moving again, in what

Morrolan thought was the right direction. We took a few tentative steps and stopped again when Aliera gasped. She said, "I can't . . ." and we let her sink to the ground.

Her breath came in gasps. She closed her eyes, her head up toward the sky; her brow was damp and her hair seemed soaked with sweat. Morrolan and I looked at each other, but no words came.

A minute or so later, as we were still standing there wondering if we would mortally insult Aliera if we offered to carry her, we saw a figure approach us out of the darkness and gradually become visible in the light of those incredible stars.

He was very tall and his shoulders were huge. There was a massive sword at his back, and his facial features were pure Dragon, as were the colors of his clothing, though their form—a peculiar formless jacket and baggy trousers tucked into darrskin boots—were rather strange. His hair was brown and curly, his eyes dark. He was—or, rather, had died at—late middle age. He had lines of thought on his forehead, lines of anger around his eyes, and the sort of jaw that made me think he kept his teeth clenched a lot.

He studied the three of us while we looked at him. I wondered what Morrolan thought of him, but I couldn't take my eyes off the Dragonlord's face to check Morrolan's expression. I felt my pulse begin to race and my knees suddenly felt weak. I had to swallow several times in quick succession.

When he finally spoke, he was addressing Aliera. "I was told I'd find you here."

She nodded but didn't say anything. She looked miserable. Morrolan, who I guess wasn't used to being ignored, said, "I greet you, lord. I am Morrolan e'Drien."

He turned to Morrolan and nodded. "Good day," he said. "I am Kieron."

Kieron.

Kieron the Conqueror.

Father of the Dragaeran Empire, elder of the proudest of lines of the House of the Dragon, hero of myth and legend, first of the great Dragaeran butchers of Easterners, and, well, I could go on, but what's the point? Here he was.

Morrolan stared at him and slowly dropped to one knee.
I didn't know where to look.

People should know better.

I don't know of any case of a Jhereg testifying to the
Empire against the Jhereg and surviving, yet there are still
fools who try. "I'm different," they say. "I've got a plan.
No one will be able to touch me; I'm protected." Or maybe
it isn't even that well thought out, maybe it's just that they're
unable to believe in their own mortality. Or else they figure
that the amount of money the Empire is paying them makes
it worth the risk.

But never mind, that isn't my problem.

I was hired through about four layers, I think. I met with
a guy in front of a grocer, and we talked as we strolled
around the block. Loiosh rode on my left shoulder. It was
early morning, and the area we were in was empty. The
guy was called "Feet" for some reason or other. I knew
who he was, and when he proposed an assassination I knew
it had to be big, because he was placed pretty high in the
Organization. That meant that whoever had told him to get
this done must be *really* important.

I told him, "I know people who do that king of thing.
Would you like to tell me about it?"

He said, "There was a problem between two friends of
ours." This meant between two Jhereg. "It got serious, and
things started getting very uncomfortable all around." This
meant that one or both of these individuals was very highly
placed in the Organization. "One of them was afraid he'd
get hurt, and he panicked and went to the Empire for protection."

I whistled. "Is he giving official testimony?"

"He already has to an extent, and he's going to give more."

"Ouch. That's going to hurt."

"We're working on burying it. We may be able to. If we
can't, things will get nasty all over for a while."

"Yeah, I imagine."

"We need serious work done. I mean, *serious* work. You
understand?"

I swallowed. "I think so, but you'd better state it clearly."

"Morganti."

"That's what I thought."

"Your friend ever done that?"

"What's the difference?"

"None, I suppose. Your friend will have the full backing of many people on this; all the support he needs."

"Yeah, I'll need some time to think about it."

"Certainly. Take as much time as you need. The price is ten thousand imperials."

"I see."

"How much time do you need to think it over?"

I was silent for a few minutes as we walked. Then I said, "Tell me his name."

"Raiet. Know him?"

"No."

We walked for a while as I thought things over. The neighborhood did neighborhood things all around us. It was a peculiar, peaceful kind of walk. I said, "All right. I'll do it."

"Good," he said. "Let's walk over to my place. I'll pay you and give you what information we have to start with. Let us know as you need more and we'll do what we can."

"Right," I said.

I found myself taking a step backward from the father of the Dragaeran Empire, while conflicting thoughts and emotions buzzed around my brain faster than I could note them. Fear and anger fought for control of my mouth, but rationality won for a change.

We held these positions for a moment. Kieron continued to look down at Aliera. Something in how they looked at each other seemed to indicate they had met before. I don't know how that could be, since Kieron was as old as the Empire and Aliera was less than a thousand years old, however you measured her age.

Kieron said, "Well, will you stand up?"

Her eyes flashed. She hissed, "No, I'm going to lie right here forever." Yes, I know there are no sibilants in what she said. I don't care; she hissed it.

Kieron chuckled. "Very well," he said. "If you ever do

decide to stand up, you may come and speak to me." He started to turn away, stopped, looked right at me. For some reason I couldn't meet his eyes. He said, "Have you anything to say to me?"

My tongue felt thick in my mouth. I could find no words. Kieron left.

Morrolan stood up. Aliera was quietly sobbing on the ground. Morrolan and I studied our belt buckles. Presently Aliera became silent; then she said in a small voice, "Please help me to rise."

We did, Morrolan indicated a direction, and we set off on our slow, limping way. Loiosh was being strangely silent. I said, *"Something bothering you, chum?"*

"I just want to get out of here, boss."

"Yeah. Me, too."

I said to Aliera, "You seemed to recognize him."

She said, "So did you."

"I did?"

"Yes."

I chewed that over for a moment, then decided not to pursue it. Presently a pair of what seemed to be monuments appeared before us. We passed between them and found ourselves back amid the thrones of the gods. We kept going without taking too close a look at the beings we'd just blithely stepped past.

A bit later Morrolan said, "Now what?"

I said, "You're asking me? Wait a minute. I just thought of something."

"Yes?"

I looked around and eventually spotted a purple robe passing by. I called out, "You. Come here."

He did, quite humbly.

I spoke to him for a moment, and he nodded back at me without speaking, his eyes lifeless. He began leading us, adjusting himself to our pace. It was a long walk and we had to stop once or twice on the way while Aliera rested.

At last we came to a throne where was seated a female figure the color of marble, with eyes like diamonds. She held a spear. The purple robe bowed to us and turned away.

The goddess said, "The living are not allowed here."

Her voice was like the ringing of chimes. It brought tears to my eyes just to hear it. It took me a moment to recover enough to say anything, in part because I'd expected Morrolan to jump in. But I said, "I am Vladimir Taltos. These are Morrolan and Aliera. You are Kelchor?"

"I am."

Morrolan handed her the disk he'd been given by the cat-centaurs. She studied it for a moment, then said, "I see. Very well, then, what do you wish?"

"For one thing, to leave," said Morrolan.

"Only the dead leave," said Kelchor. "And that, rarely."

"There is Zerika," said Morrolan.

Kelchor shook her head. "I told them it was a dangerous precedent. In any case, that has nothing to do with you."

Morrolan said, "Can you provide us with food and a place to rest while Aliera recovers her strength?"

"I can provide you with food and a place to rest," she said. "But this is the land of the dead. She will not recover her strength here."

"Even sleep would help," said Aliera.

"Those who sleep here," said Kelchor, "do not wake again as living beings. Even Easterners," she added, giving me a look I couldn't interpret.

I said, "Oh, fine," and suddenly felt very tired.

Morrolan said, "Is there any way in which you can help us?" He sounded almost like he was begging, which in other circumstances I would have enjoyed.

Kelchor addressed Aliera, saying, "Touch this." She held out her spear, just as Mist had done for me. Aliera touched it without hesitation.

I felt the pressure of holding her up ease. Kelchor raised the spear again, and Aliera said, "I thank you."

Kelchor said, "Go now."

I said, "Where?"

Kelchor opened her mouth to speak, but Aliera said, "To find Kieron."

I wanted to say that he was the last thing I wanted to see just then, but the look on Aliera's face stopped me. She let go of our support and, though she seemed a bit shaky, walked away on her own. Morrolan and I bowed low to

Kelchor, who seemed amused, then we followed Aliera.

Aliera found a purple robe and said in a loud, clear voice, "Take us to Kieron."

I hoped he'd be unable to, but he just bowed to her and began leading us off.

15 -

When I felt it, it was almost as if I heard Noish-pa's voice saying, "Now, Vladimir."

"Now, Vladimir."

It is much too long a phrase for that instant of time in which I knew to act, but that is what I recall, and that is what I responded to. It burst.

There was no holding back, there were no regrets; doubts became abstract and distant. Everything had concentrated on building to this place in time, and I was alive as I am never alive except at such moments. The exhilaration, the release, the plunge into the unknown, it was all there. And, best of all, there was no longer any point in doubting. If I was to be destroyed, it was now too late to do anything about it. Everything I'd been saving and holding back rushed forth. I felt my energy flow away as if someone had pulled the plug. It spilled forth, and, for the moment, I was far too confused to know or, for that matter, to wonder if my timing had been right. Death and madness, or success. Here it was.

My eyes snapped open and I looked upon bedlam.

• • •

Even if my life depended on it, I couldn't tell you how we ended up there, but the purple robe somehow led us back to the white hallway through which we'd approached the gods. There was a side passage in it, though I'd noticed none before, and we took it, following its curves and twists until we came to a room that was white and empty save for many candles and Kieron the Conqueror.

He stood with his back to the door and his head bowed, doing I don't know what before one of the candles. He turned as we entered and locked gazes with Aliera.

"You are standing on your own, I see."

"Yes," she said. "And now that I do so, I can explain how proud I am to be descended from one who mocks the injured."

"I am glad you're proud, Aliera e'Kieron."

She drew herself up as best she could. "Don't—"

"Do not think to instruct me," he said. "You haven't earned it."

"Are you sure?" she said. "I know you, Kieron. And if you don't know me, it's only because you're as blind as you always were."

He stared at her but allowed no muscle in his face to change. Then he looked right at me and I felt my spine turn to water. I kept it off my face. He said, "Very well, then, Aliera; what about him?"

"He isn't your concern," said Aliera.

I leaned over to Morrolan and said, "I love being spoken of as if—"

"Shut up, Vlad."

"Polite bastards, all of them."

"I know, boss."

Kieron said to Aliera, "Are you quite certain he isn't my concern?"

"Yes," said Aliera. I wished I knew what this was about.

Kieron said, "Well, then, perhaps not. Would you care to sit?"

"No," she said.

"Then what would you like?"

Her legs were still a bit unsteady as she approached him. She stopped about six inches away from him and said, "You may escort us out of the Paths, to make up for your lack of courtesy."

He started to smile, stopped. He said, "I do not choose to leave again. I have done—"

"Nothing for two hundred thousand years. Isn't that long enough?"

"It is not your place to judge—"

"Keep still. If you're determined to continue to allow history to pass you by, give me your sword. I'll fight my own way out, and put it to the use for which it was intended. You may be finished with it, but I don't think it has finished its task."

Kieron's teeth were clenched and the fires of Verra's hell burned in his gaze.

He said, "Very well, Aliera e'Kieron. If you think you can wield it, you can take it."

Now, if some of this conversation doesn't make sense to you, I can only say that it doesn't make sense to me, either. For that matter, judging from the occasional glances I took at Morrolan's face, he wasn't doing much better at understanding it than I. But I'm telling you as best I can remember it, and you'll just have to be as satisfied with it as I am.

Aliera said, "I can wield it."

"Then I charge you to use it well, and to return to this place rather than give it to another or let it be taken from you."

"And if I don't?" she said, I think just to be contrary.

"Then I'll come and take it."

"Perhaps," said Aliera, "that's what I want."

They matched stares for a little longer, then Kieron unstrapped swordbelt and sword and scabbard and passed the whole thing over to Aliera. It was quite a bit taller than she was; I wondered how she'd even be able to carry it.

She took it into her hand without appearing to have difficulty, though. When she had it she didn't even bow to Kieron, she merely turned on her heel and walked out the door, a bit shakily, but without faltering. We followed her.

"Come on," she said. "We're going home. All of us. Let him stop us who can."

It didn't sound practical, but it was still the best idea I'd heard that day.

The information Feet had "to start with" consisted of fourteen pages of parchment, all tightly written by, apparently, a professional scribe, though that seemed unlikely. It consisted of a list of Raiet's friends and how often he visited them, his favorite places to eat out and what he liked to order at each, his history in the Organization (which made this an amazingly incriminating document itself), and more like that. There was much detail about his mistress and where she lived (there's no custom against nailing someone at his mistress's place, unlike his own home). I'd never had any interest in knowing so much about someone. Toward the end were several notes such as, "Not a sorcerer. Good in a knife fight; very quick. Hardly a swordsman." This stuff ought not to matter but was good to know.

On the other hand, this made me wonder if, perhaps, this wasn't the sort of thing I should be trying to find out about all of my targets. I mean, sure, killing someone with a Morganti weapon is as serious as it gets, but any assassination is, well, a matter of life and death.

In addition to the parchment, Feet gave me a large purse containing more money than I'd ever seen in my life, most of it in fifty-imperial coins.

And he gave me a box. As soon as I touched it, I felt for the first time, albeit distantly, that peculiar hollow humming echo within the mind. I shuddered and realized just what I'd gotten myself into.

It was, of course, far too late to back out.

Tromp tromp tromp. Hear us march, ever onward, onward, doom uncertain, toward the unknown terrors of death, heads high, weapons ready . . .

What a load of crap.

We made our way through the corridors of the Halls of Judgment as well as we could, which wasn't very. What had been a single straight, wide corridor had somehow turned into a twisty maze of little passages, all the same. We must have wandered those halls for two or three hours, getting more and more lost, with none of us willing to admit it. We tried marking the walls with the points of our swords, keeping to the left-hand paths, but nothing worked. And the really odd thing was that none of the passages led anywhere except to other passages. That is, there were no rooms, stairways, doors, or anything else.

The purple robes we asked to lead us out just looked at us blankly. Aliera had buckled Kieron's greatsword onto her back and was grimly not feeling the weight. Morrolan was equally grim about not feeling anything. Neither Loiosh nor I felt like talking. No one else had any good suggestions, either. I was getting tired.

We stopped and rested, leaning against a wall. Aliera tried to sit down on the floor and discovered that the greatsword on her back made this impossible. She looked disgusted. I think she was close to tears. So was I for that matter.

We talked quietly for a while, mostly complaining. Then Morrolan said, "All right. This isn't working. We are going to have to find the gods and convince them to let us go."

"No," said Aliera. "The gods will prevent you from leaving."

"The gods do not have to prevent me from leaving; these halls are doing a quite sufficient job of that."

Aliera didn't answer.

Morrolan said, "I suspect we could wander these halls forever without finding a way out. We need to ask someone, and I, for one, can think of no better expert than Verra."

"No," said Aliera.

"Are you lost, then?" came a new voice. We turned, and there was Baritt once again. He seemed pleased. I scowled but kept my mouth shut.

"Who are you?" asked Aliera.

Morrolan said, "This is Baritt."

Baritt said, "And you?"

"I am Aliera."

His eyes widened. "Indeed? Well, this is, indeed, droll. And you are trying to return to living lands, are you not? Well then, I crave a favor. If you succeed, and I am still alive, don't visit me. I don't think I could stand it."

Aliera said, "My Lord, we are—"

"Yes, I know. I cannot help you. There is no way out except the one you know. Any purple robe can guide you back there. I am sorry."

And he did actually seem to be sorry, too, but he was looking at Aliera as he said it.

Aliera scowled and her nostrils flared. She said, "Very well, then," and we left Baritt standing there.

Finding a purple robe in that place was about as difficult as finding a Teckla in the market. And, yes, the purple robe was willing to escort us back to see the gods. She seemed to have no trouble finding the large passage. The thought crossed my mind that we could just turn around and take this passage out the way we'd come. I didn't suggest it because I had the feeling it wouldn't work.

We passed through the gate once more, the purple robe leaving us there, and we came once more before the throne of Verra, the Demon Goddess. She was smiling.

The bitch.

I could have done most of my planning without ever leaving my flat, and I almost decided to. But I was getting more and more nervous about this whole Morganti business, so I decided to take the precaution of verifying some of the information on the fact sheets.

I'll make a long, dull story short and say it all checked out, but I was happier seeing it myself. His imperially assigned protection consisted of three Dragonlords who were always with him, all of whom were very good. None of them spotted me while I was following them around, but they made me nervous. I eventually sent Loiosh to trail him while I studied the information, looking for a weakness.

The problem was the fact that the bodyguards were of the House of Dragon. Otherwise, I could probably bribe them to step out of the way at the crucial time. I wondered if the Dragons might have other weaknesses.

Well, for the moment, assume they did. Was there a good, obvious place to take him? Sure. There was a lady he liked to visit in the west of Adrilankha, past the river.

If there is a better time and place to nail someone than his mistress's, I don't know what it is. Loiosh checked the area out for me and it was perfect—rarely traveled in the early morning hours when he left her place, yet with a fair share of structures to hide near. All right, if I were going to take him there, what would I do? Replace the cabman who picked him up? That would involve bribing the cabman, who'd then know about the assassination, or else killing or disabling him, which I didn't like.

No, there had to be a better way.

And there was, and I found it.

She said, "I greet you again, mortals. And you, Aliera, I give you welcome. You may leave this place, and the Easterner may accompany you, on the condition that he never return. The Lord Morrolan will remain."

"No," said Aliera. "He returns with us."

The goddess continued to smile.

"All right," said Aliera. "Explain to me why he has to stay here."

"It is the nature of this place. The living are simply unable to return. Perhaps he can become undead, and leave that way. There are those who have managed this. I believe you know Sethra Lavode, for instance."

"That is not acceptable," said Aliera.

Verra smiled, saying nothing.

Morrolan said, "Let it lie, Aliera."

Aliera's face was hard and grim. "That's nonsense. What about Vlad, then? If it was the nature of the place, he couldn't leave either. And don't tell me it's because he's an Easterner—you know and I know there's no difference between the soul of an Easterner and the soul of a Dragaeran." Indeed? Then why weren't Easterners allowed into the Paths of the Dead, assuming we'd want to be? But this wasn't the time to ask.

Aliera continued, "I couldn't leave either, for that matter. And didn't the Empress Zerika manage? And for that matter, what about you? I know what being a Lord of Judgment means, and there's nothing that makes you so special that you should be immune to these effects. You're lying."

Verra's face lost its smile, and her multijointed hands twitched—an odd, inhuman gesture that scared me more than her presence. I expected Aliera to be destroyed on the spot, but Verra only said, "I owe you no explanation, little Dragon."

Aliera said, "Yes, you do," and Verra flushed. I wondered what it was that had passed between them.

Then Verra smiled, just a little, and said, "Yes, perhaps I do owe you an explanation. First of all, you are simply wrong. You don't know as much about being a god as you think you do. Easterners hold gods in awe, denying us any humanity. Dragaerans have the attitude that godhood is a skill, like sorcery, and there's nothing more to it than that. Neither is correct. It is a combination of many skills, and many natural forces, and involves changes in every aspect of the personality. I was never human, but if I had been, I wouldn't be now. I am a god. My blood is the blood of a god. It is for this reason that the Halls of Judgment cannot hold me.

"In the case of Zerika, she was able to leave because the Imperial Orb has power even here. Still, we could have stopped her, and we nearly did. It is no small thing to allow the living the leave this place, even those few who are capable.

"Your Easterner friend could never have come here without a living body to carry him. No, the soul doesn't matter, but it's more complicated than that. It is the blood. As a living man he could bring himself here, and as a living man he can leave." She suddenly looked at me. "Once. Don't come back, Fenarian." I tried not to look as if I were shaking.

Verra went on, "And as for you, Aliera . . . " Her voice trailed off and she smiled.

Aliera flushed and looked down. "I see."

"Yes. In your case, as perhaps your friends told you, I had some difficulty in persuading certain parties to allow you to leave. If you weren't the heir to the throne, we would have required you to stay, and your companion with you. Are you answered?"

Aliera nodded without looking up.

"What about me, boss?"

Shit. I hadn't thought of that. I screwed up my courage and said, "Goddess, I need to know—"

"Your familiar shares your fate, of course."

"Oh. Yes. Thank you."

"Thanks, boss. I feel better."

"You do?"

Verra said, "Are you ready to leave, then? You should depart soon, because if you sleep, none of you will live again, and there are imperial rules against the undead holding official imperial positions."

Aliera said, "I will not leave without my cousin."

"So be it," snapped Verra. "Then you will stay. Should you change your mind, however, the path out of here is through the arch your friends know, and to the left, past the Cycle, and onward. You may take it if you can. The Lord Morrolan will find his life seeping away from him as he walks, but he can try. Perhaps you will succeed in bringing a corpse out of this land, and denying him the repose of the Paths as well as the life which is already forfeit. Now leave me."

We looked at each other. I was feeling very tired indeed.

For lack of anywhere else to go, we went past the throne until we found the archway beneath which we'd first met Kieron the Conqueror. To the right was the path to the well, which was still tempting, but I still knew better. To the left was the way out, for Aliera and me.

I discovered, to my disgust, that I really didn't want to leave Morrolan there. If it had been Aliera who had to stay, I might have felt differently, but that wasn't one of my options. We stood beneath the arch, no one moving.

I opened the box. The sensation I'd felt upon touching it became stronger. It contained a sheathed dagger. Touching the sheath was very difficult for me. Touching the hilt was even more difficult.

"I don't like this thing, boss."

"Neither do I."

"Do you have to draw it before—"

"Yes. I need to know I can use it. Now shut up, Loiosh. You aren't making this any easier."

I drew the dagger and it assaulted my mind. I found my hand was trembling, and forced my grip to relax. I tried to study the thing as if it were just any weapon. The blade was thirteen inches, sharp on one side. It had enough of a point to be useful, but the edge was better. It had a good handguard and it balanced well. The hilt was nonreflective black, and—

Morganti.

I held it until I stopped shaking. I had never touched one of these before. I almost made a vow never to touch one again, but careless vows are stupid, so I didn't.

But it was a horrible thing to hold, and I never did get used to it. I knew there were those who regularly carried them, and I wondered if they were sick, or merely made of better stuff than I.

I forced myself to take a few cuts and thrusts with it. I set up a pine board so I could practice thrusting it into something. I held it the whole time, using my left hand to put the board against a wall on top of a dresser. I held my right hand, with the knife, rigidly out to the side away from my left hand. I must have looked absurd, but Loiosh didn't laugh. I could tell he was exercising great courage in not flying from the room.

Well, so was I, for that matter.

I thrust it into the board about two dozen times, forcing myself to keep striking until I relaxed a bit, until I could treat it as just a weapon. I never fully succeeded, but I got closer. When I finally resheathed the thing, I was drenched with sweat and my arm was stiff and sore.

I put it back in its box.

"Thanks, boss. I feel better."

"Me, too. Okay. Everything is set for tomorrow. Let's get some rest."

As we stood, I said to Aliera, "So tell me, what's so special about you that you can leave here and Morrolan can't?"

"It's in the blood," she said.

"Do you mean that, or is it a figure of speech?"

She looked at me scornfully. "Take it however you will."

"Ummm, would you like to be more specific?"

"No," said Aliera.

I shrugged. At least she hadn't told me she owed me no explanation. I was getting tired of that particular phrase. Before us was a wall, and paths stretched out to the right and to the left. I looked to the right.

I said, "Morrolan, do you know anything about that water Verra drank and fed to Aliera?"

"Very little," he said.

"Do you think it might allow us to—"

"No," said Aliera and Morrolan in one voice. I guess they knew more about it than I did, which wasn't difficult. They didn't offer any explanations and I didn't press the issue. We just stood for a long moment, then Morrolan said, "I think there is no choice. You must go. Leave me here."

"No," said Aliera.

I chewed on my lower lip. I couldn't think of anything to say. Then Morrolan said, "Come. Whatever we decide, I wish to look upon the Cycle."

Aliera nodded. I had no objection.

We took the path to the left.

16 -

The horizon jumped and twisted, the candle exploded, the knife vibrated apart, and the humming became, in an instant, a roar that deafened me.

On the ground before me, the rune glowed like to blind me, and I realized that I was feeling very sleepy. I knew what that meant, too. I had no energy left to even keep me awake. I was going to lose consciousness, and I might or might not ever regain it, and I might or not be mad if I did.

My vision wavered, and the roar in my ears became a single monotone that was, strangely, the same as silence. In the last blur before I slipped away, I saw on the ground, in the center of the rune, the object of my desire—that which I'd done all of this to summon—sitting placidly, as if it had been there all along.

I wondered, for an instant, why I was taking no joy in my success; then I decided that it probably had something to do with not knowing if I'd live to use it. But there was still somewhere the sense of triumph for having done something no witch had ever done before, and a certain serene pleasure in having succeeded. I decided I'd feel pretty good if it didn't kill me.

Dying, I've found, always puts a crimp in my enjoyment of an event.

I'd love to see a map of the Paths of the Dead.

Ha.

We followed the wall to the left, and it kept circling around until we ought to have been near the thrones, but we were still in a hallway with no ceiling. The stars vanished sometime in thee, leaving a grey overcast, yet there was no lessening in the amount of light I thought had been provided by the stars. I dunno.

The wall ended and we seemed to be on a cliff overlooking a sea. There was no sea closer than a thousand miles to Deathgate Falls, but I suppose I ought to have stopped expecting geographical consistency some time before.

We stared out at the dark, gloomy sea for a while and listened to its roar. It stretched out forever, in distance and in time. I can't look at a sea, even the one at home, without wondering about who lives beyond it. What sorts of lives do they have? Better than ours? Worse? So similar I couldn't tell the difference? So different I couldn't survive there? What would it be like? How did they live? What sorts of beds did they have? Were they soft and warm, like mine, safe and—

"Vlad!"

"Uh, what?"

"We want to get moving," said Morrolan.

"Oh. Sorry. I'm getting tired."

"I know."

"Okay, let's— Wait a minute."

I reached around and opened my pack, dug around amid the useless witchcraft supplies I'd carried all this way, and found some kelsch leaves. I passed them around. "Chew on these," I said.

We all did so, and, while nothing remarkable or exciting happened, I realized that I was more awake. Morrolan smiled. "Thanks, Vlad."

"I should have thought of it sooner."

"I should have thought of it, boss. That's my job. Sorry."

"You're tired, too. Want a leaf? I've got another."

"No, thanks. I'll get by."

We looked around, and far off to our right was what seemed to be a large rectangle. We headed toward it. As we got closer, it resolved itself into a single wall about forty feet high and sixty feet across. As we came still closer, we could see there was a large circular object mounted on its face. My pulse quickened.

Moments later the three of us stood contemplating the Cycle of the Dragaeran Empire.

Raiet picked up a carriage at the Imperial Palace the next day and went straight to the home of his mistress. A Dragon-lord rode with him, another rode next to the driver, and a third, on horseback, rode next to the carriage, or in front of it, or behind it. Loiosh flew above it, but that wasn't part of their arrangements.

Watching them through my familiar's eyes, I had to admire their precision, futile though it was. The one on top of the coach got down first, checked out the area, and went straight into the building and up to the flat, which was on the second floor of the three-story brick building.

If you'd been there watching, you would have seen the rider dismount smartly as the driver got down and held the door for the two inside while looking up and down the street, and up at the rooftops as well. Raiet and the two Dragons walked into the building together. The first one was already inside the flat and had checked it over. Raiet's mistress, who name was Treffa, nodded to the Dragon and continued setting out chilled wine. She seemed a bit nervous as she went about this, but she'd been growing more and more nervous as this testimony business continued.

As he finished checking the apartment, the other two Dragons delivered Raiet. Treffa smiled briefly and brought the wine into the bedchamber. He turned to one of the Dragons and shook his head. "I think she's getting tired of this."

The Dragon probably shrugged; he'd been assigned to protect a Jhereg, but he didn't have to like it, or him, and I assume he didn't. Raiet walked into the bedchamber and closed the door. Treffa walked over to the door and did something to it.

"What's that, babe?"

"A soundproofing spell. I just bought it."

He chuckled. "They making you nervous?"

She nodded.

"I suppose it's starting to wear on you."

She nodded again and poured them each a glass of wine.

When he hadn't appeared after his usual few hours, the Dragons knocked on the door. When no one answered, they broke the door down. They found his lifeless and soulless body on the bed, a Morganti knife buried in his chest. They wondered why they hadn't heard him scream, or the window opening. Treffa lay next to him, drugged and unconscious. They couldn't figure out how the drugs had gotten into the wine, and Treffa was no help with any of it.

They were suspicious of her, naturally, but were never able to prove that Treffa had actually taken money to set him up. She disappeared a few months later and is doing quite well to this day, and Treffa isn't her name anymore, and I won't tell you where she's living.

It is commonly believed that if anyone had the strength to take hold of the great wheel that is the Cycle and physically move it, the time of the current House would pass, and the next would arrive. It is also commonly held that it would require enough strength to overcome all the weight contained by the forces of history, tradition, and will that keep the Cycle turning as it does. This being the case, it seems a moot point, especially when, as I stared at it, it was hard to imagine anyone with the strength to just move the bloody great wheel.

That's all it was, too. A big wheel stuck onto a wall in the middle of nowhere. On the wheel were engraved symbolic represenations of all seventeen Houses. The Phoenix was at the top, the Dragon next in line, the Athyra having just passed. What a thrill it must be to be here when it actually changed, signaling the passing of another phase of Dragaeran history. At that point, either the Empress would step down, or she would have recently done so, or would soon do so, or perhaps she would refuse and blood would run in the Empire until the political and the mystical were once more in agreement. When would it happen? Tomorrow? In a thousand years?

Everyone I've asked insists that this thing *is* the Cycle in every meaningful way, not merely its physical manifestation. I can't make sense of that, but if you can, more power to you, so to speak.

I glanced at Morrolan and Aliera, who also stared at the Cycle, awe on their faces.

"Boss, the kelsch won't last forever."

"Right, Loiosh. Thanks."

I said, "All right, folks. Whatever we're going to do, we'd best be about it."

They looked at me, at each other, at the ground, then back at the Cycle. None of us knew what to do. I turned my back on them and walked back to look out over the sea again.

I won't say that I'm haunted by the look in Raiet's eyes in that last moment—when the Morganti dagger struck him—or his scream as his soul was destroyed. He deserved what happened to him, and that's that.

But I never got used to touching that weapon. It's the ultimate predator, hating everything, and it would have been as happy to destroy me as Raiet. Morganti weapons scare me right down to my toes, and I'm never going to be happy dealing with them. But I guess it's all part of the job.

The whole thing gave me a couple of days of uneasy conscience in any case, though. Not, as I say, for Raiet; but somehow this brought home to me a thought that I'd been ignoring for over a year: I was being paid money to kill people.

No, I was being paid money to kill Dragaerans; Dragaerans who had made my life miserable for more than seventeen years. Why shouldn't I let them make my life pleasant instead? Loiosh, I have to say, was no help at all in this. He had the instincts of an eater of carrion and sometime hunter.

I really didn't know if I was creating justifications that would eventually break down or not. But a couple of days of wondering was all I could take. I managed to put it out of my mind, and, to be frank, it hasn't bothered me since.

I don't know, maybe someday it will, and if so I'll deal with it then.

I don't know how long I stood there, perhaps an hour, before Morrolan and Aliera came up behind me. Then the three of us watched the waves break for a few minutes. Behind us, the way we'd come, were the Paths of the Dead and the Halls of Judgment. To our right, beyond the Cycle, was a dark forest, through which lay the way out, for some of us.

After a time Aliera said, "I won't leave without Morrolan."

Morrolan said, "You are a fool."

"And you're another for coming here when you knew you couldn't get out alive."

"I can think of another fool, Loiosh."

"Another two, boss."

"That's as may be," said Morrolan. "But there is no need to make the venture useless."

"Yes there is. I choose to do so."

"It is absurd to kill yourself merely because—"

"It is what I will do. No one, *no one* will sacrifice his life for me. I won't have it. We both leave, or we both remain."

There was a cool breeze on the right side of my face. That way was home. I shook my head. Morrolan should have known better than to expect rationality from a Dragaeran, much less a Dragonlord. But then, he was one himself.

Aliera said, "Go back, Vlad. I thank you for your help, but your task is finished."

Yes, Morrolan was a Dragonlord and a Dragaeran. He was also pompous and abrasive as hell. So why did I feel such a resistance to just leaving him? But what else could I do? There was no way to leave with him, and I, at least, saw no value in pointless gestures.

Morrolan and Aliera were looking at me. I looked away.

"Leave, Vlad," said Morrolan. I didn't move.

"You heard him, boss. Let's get out of here."

I stood there yet another minute. I wanted to be home, but the notion of just saying good-bye to Morrolan and walking away, well, I don't know. It didn't feel right.

I've spent many fruitless minutes since then wondering what would have happened if the breeze hadn't shifted just then, bringing with it the tang of salt and the smell of seaweed.

Dead bodies and seaweed. I chuckled. Yeah, this was a place where that phrase was appropriate. Where had I first heard it? Oh, yeah, the bar. Ferenk's. Drinking with Kiera.

Kiera. Right. That. It just might do it. If there was only a way . . .

Witchcraft?

I looked at Morrolan and Aliera.

"It's crazy, boss."

"I know. But still—"

"We don't even know if we're on the same world as—"

"Maybe it doesn't matter."

"What if it does?"

"Boss, do you have any idea how much that will take out of you?"

"They'll have to carry me back."

"If it doesn't work, they won't be able to."

"I know."

Loiosh shut up, as he realized I wasn't really listening to him. I dug in my pack and found my last kelsch leaf.

Aliera said, "What is it, Vlad?"

"An idea for getting Morrolan out of here. Will you two be willing to carry me if I can't walk on my own?"

Morrolan said, "What is it?"

"Witchcraft," I said.

"How—"

"I'm going to have to invent a spell. I'm not certain it can be done."

"I am a witch. Can I help?"

I hesitated, then shook my head. "I have one more kelsch leaf left. I'm going to chew on it myself in order to get the energy to do the spell. If you help, who will carry us both out?"

"Oh. What is the spell intended to do?"

I licked my lips, realizing that I didn't want to tell him.

"Why not, boss?"

"He'll just say it can't be done."

"Well, can it?"

"We'll find out."

"Why?"

"I've always wanted to test myself as a witch. Here's my big chance."

"Boss, I'm serious. If you put that much into it and it doesn't work it will—"

"Kill me. I know. Shut up."

"And with the amount of energy you'll have to pour into it you won't be able to stay awake. And—"

"Drop it, Loiosh."

To Morrolan I said, "Never mind. Wait here. I'm going to find a place to set this up. I'll probably be near the Cycle, so stay away from there; I don't want anyone around to distract me. When I'm done, if it works, I'll find you."

"What if it doesn't work?"

"Then you'll find me."

Bribing Treffa had cost quite a bit, as had the soundproofing spells and the escape, since I dealt directly with a sorceress who worked for the Left Hand, rather than going through Feet. Why? I don't know. I mean, after hiring me, he wouldn't turn around and shine me after I did the job. If word of that got around, no one would work for him again. But on the other hand, this killling was *Morganti*. If he had the chance to cleanly dispose of me by having a teleport go wrong, he *probably* wouldn't take it, but why tempt him?

In any case, by the time all was said and done, I'd spent a great deal, but I still had a great deal left. I decided not to live it up this time, because I didn't want to call attention to myself. I didn't want to leave town for the same reason. This killing made quite a splash, and that made me nervous, but I got over it.

So far as I know, no one ever found out I'd done it. But once again, there were those who seemed to know. One of them was Welok the Blade, who was about as nasty as they

come. I started working directly for him a few weeks later—
doing collecting and trouble-shooting and keeping an eye
on his people. I carefully set aside the money I'd earned,
determined to invest it in something that would keep earning
for me. Maybe even something legitimate.

About a month after I started working for Welok, I was
visiting my grandfather in South Adrilankha, and I met a
human girl named Ibronka, who had the longest, straightest,
blackest hair I'd ever seen, and eyes you could get lost in.
I still hadn't made my investment.

Oh, well.

After going this far, I couldn't back out. The three of us
were going to leave together or not at all, and now there
was a chance of success. If I'd wanted to pray just then, I
would have prayed to my grandfather, not to Verra, because
his guidance would have been more useful.

I didn't think he'd ever tried inventing a spell, though.
Dammit, if sorcery worked around here, Morrolan could
have simply caused the thing to appear from my flat. But
then, if sorcery worked we could have just teleported out
of here. No point in thinking about that.

I selected a spot facing the Cycle. Why? I'm not sure. It
seemed appropriate, and the apropos is a vital thing to a
practicing witch.

I started chewing on the leaf while I meditated, relaxing,
preparing myself. When it had done as much for me as it
was capable of, I spit it out.

I took my pack off and opened it, then sat down. I wondered if the gods would stop me, then decided that if they
were looking at me, they would have done something as
soon as I began laying out the implements of the spell. It
was amusing to be out of their sight, yet right in their
backyard, so to speak.

I studied the Cycle and tried to collect my courage.

Waiting would just make things more difficult.

I took a deep breath and began the spell.

17 -

I have a vague memory of a little girl shaking my shoulder, saying, "Don't fall asleep. You'll die if you fall asleep. Stay awake."

When I opened my eyes there was no one there, so it may have been a dream. On the other hand, to dream one must be sleeping, and if I was sleeping . . .

I don't know.

Flap flap, peck peck.

I knew what that was. My eyes opened. I spoke aloud. "It's all right. I'm back."

I don't think I've ever had to work so hard to stand up. When I'd finally managed, I felt the way Aliera must have, and I really wished I had more kelsch leaves to chew on. The world spun around and around. Don't you just hate it when it does that?

I started walking, then heard something, very distant. It gradually got more urgent in tone, so I stopped and listened. It was Loiosh, saying, *"Boss! Boss! They're back the other way."*

I got myself turned around, which wasn't as easy as you might think, and stumbled off in the direction Loiosh told me was the right one. After what seemed like hours I found them, sitting where I'd left them. Morrolan noticed me first, and I saw him moving toward me. All of his actions seemed slowed down, as did Aliera's as she rose and came toward me. I started to fall, which also seemed to happen slowly, and then the two of them were supporting me.

"Vlad, are you all right?"

I mumbled something and held on to them.

"Vlad? Did it work?"

Work? Did what work? Oh, yes. I had more to do. Wait, the vial . . . no, I had it in my hand. Good move, Vlad. I held it up. A dark, dark liquid in a clear vial with a rubber stopper.

"What is it?" asked Aliera.

Formulating an answer seemed much too difficult. I gathered my strength, looked at Morrolan, and said, "Bare your arm."

"Which one?" he asked.

I shook my head, so he shrugged and bared his left arm.

"Knife," I said.

Morrolan and Aliera exchanged looks and shrugs, and then Morrolan put a knife into my left hand. I gestured for him to come closer and, with some hesitation, he did.

I forced my hand to remain steady as I cut his biceps. I handed the vial to Aliera and said, "Open." I couldn't bring myself to watch her, though I did curse myself for not having had her open it before I cut Morrolan.

I have no idea how she managed it without letting me fall, but she did, and after a while she said, "It's done."

I grabbed Morrolan's arm and held the vial against the cut. I told him, "You're a witch. Make the liquid go into your arm."

He looked at me, puzzled, then licked his lips. I suddenly realized that he was deciding whether he trusted me. If I'd had the strength, I'd have laughed. *Him* wondering if he should trust *me*? But I guess he decided to, and he also chose to assume I knew what I was doing. More fool he on that point, I thought to myself. My eyes closed. Aliera shook me and I opened them. When I looked up, the vial was empty and Morrolan was holding it in his hand, staring at it with a mildly inquiring expression. I hoped Kiera hadn't needed it for anything important.

"Let's go home," I said.

"Vlad," asked Morrolan, "just what was that?"

"Home," I managed. There was a pause, during which they might have been looking at each other. Then, each with an arm around me, we set off for the woods.

I can't recall making a decision to set up on my own. I was in a certain situation, and I got out of it the best way I could.

The situation?

Well, when the war between Welok and Rolaan finally ended, there were a number of shakedowns. Nielar, my first boss, got rid of most of what he owned because he would have had to fight to keep it and didn't think he could manage. I respect that. Courage is all well and good, but you can't earn when you're dead, and it takes a certain kind of intelligence to know when to back off.

I had many different employers in the months after Nielar, but when everything settled down I was working for a guy named Tagichatn, or Takishat, or something like that; I've never been able to get his name exactly right.

In any case, I never liked him and he never liked me. Most of my earnings were straight commissions for collections and such, and those came pretty rarely around then. I did a few assassinations for people to whom my reputation had spread, which kept me living comfortably, but assassinations also pull in a lot of pressure; I like to have income that comes from things that aren't quite so risky.

I could have left and found employment with someone else, but I'd only been around for a few years by then and I didn't know that many people. So the best way out of the situation turned out to be killing Tagijatin.

Keep walking. Stay awake.

A dim glow seemed to come from the ground, or perhaps from the air around us, I don't know. It was almost enough light to see by. How long were we walking through that forest? Who can say? My time sense was completely screwed up by then.

Stay awake. Keep walking.

From time to time we'd stop, and Aliera and Morrolan would have a hushed conversation about which way to go. I think they were afraid we were walking in circles. When this happened Loiosh would say, *"Tell them that way, boss,"* and I'd gesture in the indicated direction. I guess by this time they were trusting me. The gods alone know why.

At one point Morrolan said, "I feel odd."

Aliera said, "What is it?"

"I'm not sure. Something strange."

"Vlad, what did you give him?"

I shook my head. Talking was just too much work. Besides, what had I given him? Oh, right. The blood of a goddess, according to Kiera. Why had I done it? Because the only other choice was letting Morrolan die.

Well, so what? What had he ever done for me? He'd saved my life, but that was because I was working for him. Friend? Nonsense. Not a Dragaeran. Not a Dragonlord, in any case.

Then why? It didn't matter; it was over. And I was too tired to think about it, anyway.

Keep walking. Stay awake.

Later, Aliera said, "I'm beginning to feel it, too. Want to rest?"

Morrolan said, "If we stop, Vlad will fall asleep, and we'll lose him."

That seemed like sufficient answer for Aliera, which surprised me. But then, why were they working so hard to save me? And why had I been so certain they would? They were Dragonlords and I was a Jhereg; they were Dragaerans and I was human. I couldn't make it make sense.

Aliera said, "How are you feeling?"

I couldn't answer, but it turned out she was speaking to Morrolan. He said, "I'm not certain how to describe it. It's as if I am lighter and heavier at the same time, and the air tastes different. I wonder what he gave me?"

"If we get out of this," said Aliera, "we can ask him later."
Stay awake. Keep walking.
The woods went on and on and on.

Killing Tadishat may have been one of the easiest things I've ever done. For someone who accumulated enemies as quickly as he did, you'd think he'd have taken some sort of precaution. But he was new at running an area, and I guess he was one of those people who think, "It can't happen to me."

I got news for you, sucker: It can.

He always worked late, doing his own bookkeeping so he could be sure no one was cheating him out of a copper, and I just walked in one day while he was poring over the books and crept up on him with a stiletto in my hand. He didn't notice me until I was right in front of him, by which time it was much too late. No problem.

By the time his body was found, I'd already moved into his office. Why? I don't know. I guess I just decided I'd rather work for me than for anyone else I could think of.

I can't recall when we left the woods, but I do remember being carried through a cave. Morrolan tells me I pointed the way to it, so I don't know. The next clear memory I have is lying on my back staring up at the orange-red Dragaeran sky and hearing Morrolan say, "Okay, I know where we are."

A teleport must have followed that, but I have no memory of it, which is just as well.

Kragar joined me right away when I took over from Tagi-chatin and, to my surprise and pleasure, Nielar showed more loyalty to me than I would have expected from a former boss. Of course, I had some problems getting started, as there were several people in my organization who had trouble taking an Easterner seriously as a boss.

I changed their minds without killing any of them, which

I think was quite an accomplishment. In fact, I didn't have any major problems running my area—until a certain button-man named Quion had to ruin it all.

Sethra Lavode, the Enchantress, the Dark Lady of Dzur Mountain, studied me from beneath her lashes. I wondered why she hadn't asked what I'd given Morrolan, and decided that she either guessed what it was or knew I wouldn't answer. I was feeling belligerent, though I'm not sure why. Maybe it had something to do with having been assisted out of the Paths of the Dead by Morrolan and Aliera, I don't know.

These two worthies were watching Sethra's face as they concluded the tale. We were sitting, quite comfortably, in the library at Dzur Mountain. Chaz served wine and blinked a lot and loudly sucked his lips.

"I am pleased," said Sethra at last. "Aliera, your presence is required by the Empire."

"So I'm given to understand," said Aliera.

"What are the rest of us, roast kethna?"

"Shut up, Loiosh," I said, though I tended to share his sentiments.

"And, Vlad," continued Sethra, "I am in your debt. And I don't say that lightly. If you think this can't help you, you are a fool."

Morrolan said, "She speaks for me, also."

I said, "That I'm a fool?"

He didn't answer. Aliera said, "I owe you something, too. Perhaps someday I'll pay you."

I licked my lips. Was there a threat in there? If so, why? They were all looking at me, except for Chaz, who seemed to be looking for insects in a corner. I didn't know what to say, so I said, "Fine. Can I go home now?"

I recovered most of the money Quion had taken, so I guess that worked out all right. I don't think it's hurt my reputation any. I've seen Morrolan a couple of times since then, and he's okay for a Dragaeran. He suggested getting together with Sethra and Aliera a few times, but I think I'll pass for the moment.

I told Kiera I'd lost the bottle, but, oddly enough, she didn't seem disturbed. I never *have* told Morrolan what was in it. Whenever he asks, I just smile and look smug. I don't know, maybe I'll tell him one of these days. Then again, maybe not.

BESTSELLING
Science Fiction
and
Fantasy

☐ 0-441-77924-7	**THE STAINLESS STEEL RAT,** Harry Harrison	$2.95
☐ 0-441-11773-2	**COUNT ZERO,** William Gibson	$2.95
☐ 0-441-16025-5	**DORSAI!,** Gordon R. Dickson	$3.50
☐ 0-441-48499-9	**LITTLE MYTH MARKER,** Robert Asprin	$2.95
☐ 0-441-87332-4	**THE WARLOCK UNLOCKED,** Christopher Stasheff	$3.50
☐ 0-441-05495-1	**BERSERKER,** Fred Saberhagen	$2.95
☐ 0-441-79977-9	**TECKLA,** Steven Brust	$2.95
☐ 0-441-58635-X	**NORBY: ROBOT FOR HIRE (The Norby Chronicles Book II),** Janet and Isaac Asimov	$2.95
☐ 0-425-10059-6	**CALLAHAN'S SECRET,** Spider Robinson	$2.95
☐ 0-441-05636-9	**BEYOND SANCTUARY,** Janet Morris	$3.50
☐ 0-441-02314-2	**A NIGHT IN THE NETHERHELLS,** Craig Shaw Gardner	$2.95

Please send the titles I've checked above. Mail orders to:

BERKLEY PUBLISHING GROUP
390 Murray Hill Pkwy., Dept. B
East Rutherford, NJ 07073

NAME _____

ADDRESS _____

CITY _____

STATE _____ ZIP _____

Please allow 6 weeks for delivery.
Prices are subject to change without notice.

POSTAGE & HANDLING:
$1.00 for one book, $.25 for each
additional. Do not exceed $3.50.

BOOK TOTAL	$_____
SHIPPING & HANDLING	$_____
APPLICABLE SALES TAX (CA, NJ, NY, PA)	$_____
TOTAL AMOUNT DUE	$_____

PAYABLE IN US FUNDS.
(No cash orders accepted.)